IN DEFENCE OF THE ACT

Effie Black

époque press

Published by époque press in 2023
www.epoquepress.com

Typeset in Paralucent Light/Light Italic &
Citrus Gothic Shadow Italic.
Typesetting & cover design by Ten Storeys®

Printed and bound in Great Britain by Clays Ltd,
Elcograf S.p.A.

British Library Cataloguing-in-Publication Data
A catalogue record for this book is available from
the British Library.

ISBN 978-1-7391881-4-6 (Paperback Edition)

Effie Black is a London based writer with a background in science. She enjoys writing from a queer perspective and she likes bringing a spot of science into her fiction too. Effie's short stories have appeared in Litro and the époque press é-zine.

In Defence of the Act is Effie's debut novel.

A FABLE

The blonde woman, who I'm pretty sure said her name is Amy but who doesn't really look like an Amy, more like an Anne, peers out at us in our rows.

'What does resilience mean to you?' she says.

No one speaks. She starts slowly pacing the width of the room, back and forth.

'Feel free to shout out.' Everyone feels free. No one shouts out.

'Anyone?'

No one.

Amy-Anne begins looking a little desperate. She tries making eye contact with each and every one of us in turn to guilt us into speech. When she gets to me, I avoid her gaze.

'What do we *mean* when we say resilience?' Her voice has started to quiver, but she maintains her fixed smile.

Dread builds in my stomach. *Please* will someone answer her? Am *I* going to have to answer her? I really would rather not. But of course, like everyone else in this room, I do know the answer. Why won't someone just tell Amy-Anne what resilience means?

Finally, a quiet voice from behind me bleats something. Amy-Anne's relief is palpable.

'What was that?' she asks eagerly.

'Umm, I think resilience is all about being strong in tough times. Bouncing back. Sort of thing.' The voice repeats, louder now.

I look back to see the speaker is a sheepish middle-aged woman, clearly a nicer woman than I, surely moved to answer out of sympathy. I try to thank her with my eyes, but I don't really know how to do that, so I probably fail.

'Bouncing back? Yes, lovely, lovely.' Amy-Anne replies, and then proceeds to offer various definitions of resilience, outlining what dictionaries, psychologists, and Buddhist monks have to say on the matter. She provides not one but two quotes from retired US basketball sensation Michael Jordan. Amy-Anne doesn't look like a basketball fan. Did she think this small room of early-career British academics would be basketball fans? Although I can only authoritatively speak for myself, I suspect she may have misjudged us. In fairness though, it does seem Mr Jordan has some sensible ideas; failure being the key to success, his missed shots and lost games spurring him on to work harder, etc. etc. etc.

Now Amy-Anne wants to share her absolute favourite definition. To do this she says she must show us an animated video, and requests that we please give her a moment to set it up. She fiddles with her laptop for a bit. The fiddling is normal fiddling at first; it always takes time to pull up a video. But it's clear to everyone when after a few moments the fiddling switches from normal fiddling to panicked fiddling. The embedded video isn't working.

'That's ok. I'll just go to the video directly on YouTube, this animation really is worth seeing,' she assures us.

But YouTube isn't loading because the laptop isn't connected to the conference hotel's Wi-Fi. We watch Amy-Anne try and fail to connect several times.

'The guest login was working earlier,' she tells us.

People are shifting in their seats. The nice middle-aged answering woman behind me is one of the many now letting out not-so-nice sighs. Quiet chatter begins at the back of the room and spreads forward. The quiet chatter grows to become simply chatter, and then starts to verge

2

on rather loud chatter.

Eventually a technical person steps in to help. I feel relieved at first, but quickly realise this is far worse. With the technical *expert* now taking over the fiddling, Amy-Anne is left at a loose end, staring out at us, murmuring apologies and reassurances. Things have gone from boring to awkward. She makes a joke about how perfect it is that in this session about resilience her own resilience is being tested right in front of us. No one laughs. I feel sorry that no one laughs, even out of simple kindness. Yet I myself remain markedly not laughing. Something about Amy-Anne makes it difficult to be kind to her. I ponder how someone can possibly become a professional public speaker without being terribly good at public speaking. But then I remember I am a scientist who isn't terribly good at science, so all things are possible.

Finally the tech hand gives a guilty shake of his head. No video today. Amy-Anne is in a tough spot, but teaching the course through example, she bounces back. She decides to simply tell us the story instead. She leans back on the desk at the front and begins. She stumbles with the tale. A lot. She has to re-start it a few times. I can't be the only one in the room wondering how many times Amy-Anne's actually watched the video she wanted so desperately to show us. She must have watched it at least once, of course. But maybe only once. Anyway, this is the gist. One day a daughter was complaining to her mother. She had so many troubles and they just kept on coming. It was making her too sad to function. There seemed nothing she could do, she was at her wit's end. Her mother beckoned her into the kitchen and told her to watch as she put three saucepans of water on the stove until the water was boiling. In one she placed a carrot, in one an egg, and in one a coffee bean. Her daughter understandably didn't know what the hell was going on. But after a while the mother asked her to take the carrot out of the water and tell her what she saw. What she saw was a boiled carrot. Then the daughter took out the egg and saw a boiled egg. Same with the coffee bean. The mother explained that the carrot, the egg and the coffee bean had all suffered the same adversity: the boiling water. The carrot had responded to this adversity by becoming soft and mushy. The struggle had transformed it from hard to fragile, anyone could smush it now. The egg responded by growing tough. It looked the same from the outside, but its heart had hardened to the world. But look at the little coffee bean! It too had entered the boiling water, yet it had come out unchanged. Not only that, the mother said, as she sipped the resulting coffee, the bean had changed the water.

The rest of the *Honing your resilience* session flies by in a blur of small group sharing, personal goal setting, and mindfulness training involving staring at and eating a single raisin for an inordinate amount of time, none of which leaves much of an impression on me. But I do emerge knowing three things:

1. Amy-Anne's name is actually Annie. It said so on the final slide. It fits her perfectly.
2. I will never try to use a video in a presentation. Ever.
3. I'd love to be a coffee bean. But I'm a complete and utter egg.

AN AWAKENING

What's your first memory? Not one of those snippet memories; a flashing image, a déjà-vu type physical sensation, a snatched sentence. What's your first *full* memory? One you recall from beginning to end? One you truly inhabit as a sentient being? One you can jump into at any point, fast forward and rewind, and play over and over in your head? Maybe I've told you this already, but here's mine.

I'm four years old. My mother is pregnant with my younger brother. Pregnancy is making her tired and boring, and her growing stomach means I can't sit on her lap anymore. Her exhaustion has reached such an extreme that on this particular Saturday morning she has entrusted me with a phenomenally important task. She has given in to my demands to be taken to the park, and as it will be my father who'll drive us, she's asked *me* to deliver a cup of tea to wake him up. Clearly my insistence that I'm old enough to help with childcare responsibilities when the new baby arrives has finally been taken on board. If I do this correctly, maybe my suggestion of not starting school in September will be considered more seriously. What a fantastic opportunity to prove my worth.

My mother hands me the mug of tea and her faith. It's a large blue mug, and in retrospect I will think it's been a little overfilled, given the context. I have no problem carrying it from the kitchen through the living

5

room to the bottom of the stairs. It's there that the issues begin. I've been holding my charge in two hands until now, clasping both hands around its body. Now I stand looking up at the more demanding terrain of the towering staircase. I slowly manoeuvre the mug, inching it around in my hands, until I'm able to grasp the handle with my right hand, and take the banister with my left. I confidently mount the first couple of steps without much thought. But a hot splash on my right foot halts my progress. The vessel is so large and full that I'm finding it difficult to keep it completely level with one hand. Only a small amount of tea has escaped so far, but I can't continue like this.

I stop and strategise. I could admit defeat and head back down the steps, probably walking backwards, and remain holding the banister with minimal spillage. Or I could attempt a journey with both hands on the mug. Both hands on the mug of course means no hands on the banister. I don't want to surrender the safety of the banister, but I don't want to abandon my quest either and I can't think of any other way. I need to fulfil my duty. I muster up all the courage I have, and let go of the banister, hovering my left hand over it for a little while, just in case. When after a few seconds I don't fall, I move my hand towards the mug and support it from the left. Much better mug-wise, but I always – and will always, even as an adult – feel a little dizzy standing still on a step without holding the banister, so I better get moving.

I hold the mug before me at eye-level, taking each step slowly and steadily. Although it threatens to, I ensure no tea spills. And I make good progress, even if I do say so myself. Feeling confident now, I start imagining the smile on my dad's face when he sees what I've achieved. If there's one thing my dad loves, it's tea, so I'm overjoyed to be the delivery girl.

Until another issue arises. The tea has now thoroughly warmed the thin-walled mug, and the mug has thoroughly warmed my cold chubby little left hand. My mum says if I want to warm my hands I need to put some bloody socks on. This doesn't make much sense to me. But it seems holding a mug of tea also does the trick, and rather too well. The warming of my left hand was a nice sensation at first. But then it moved into uncomfortable, and now painful territory. I'm supporting the mug with as little of my hand as I can, just the fingertips, but even that is getting unsustainable. Hot needles are entering my fingers and my brain is clouding with panic. I stop again, ordering myself not to look back down the stairs, and I swiftly switch hands. My left hand now has some respite on the handle, and I carry on my journey.

I have to do the ol' switcheroo a couple more times to save my fingers, but eventually I make it to the small landing at the top of the stairs. I rotate ninety degrees to the left without taking my eyes off the tea, ascend the final two steps to the main landing, and then rotate ninety degrees again. At the end of the landing is my dad's room. The destination is in sight. I don't yet know that it's unusual for my mum and dad to have separate rooms. I'll realise that when I start school, and I'll quickly learn to keep quiet about it. As I walk towards my dad's door, I allow myself to peek through the banister to my left and look down on the stairs I've scaled, feeling proud and dizzy at the same time.

When I reach my dad's room I shift the mug to one hand, being extra mindful to hold it steady. This hurts my wrist a little, but it will only be temporary. Plus I hardly notice the pain. Now the worst of the journey is over, my intense concentration has been replaced by excited anticipation. My dad is going to be so surprised! I'll knock and he'll be annoyed because he'll think it's just Mum waking him up earlier than she's supposed to, but it'll actually be me: his favourite little girl bringing him his favourite thing in the world, tea. I can't wait to see the smile on his face. I bet he'll let me climb into bed while he yawns too loudly and drinks his tea, and maybe he'll even tell me a story. I have to restrain myself from simply shouting out to him through the door. I feel like I'm going to burst.

I knock quietly at first as I don't want to annoy him, and I listen. When there's no response I knock louder, and then louder still. No reply. Although this dents my excitement somewhat, it doesn't shock me. My dad is a heavy sleeper and he wears earplugs all of the time. I once heard his sister, my auntie, say the earplugs thing is incredibly antisocial, but he

7

didn't seem to hear her. Rather than shout and ruin the surprise, I decide to sneak in.

I enter the room, and there he is sleeping deeply, making a small snoring sound. I stand in front of him, proud and beaming, holding out my steaming offering. I say, 'wakey, wakey Dad, rise and shine!' I say it louder. And then louder again. But he really must have his earplugs in tightly today because he doesn't stir. I carefully place the mug on top of a low bookshelf. As I set it down a little tea drips over the edge and onto the wood. I check behind me to see if he's woken and I'm relieved to note he hasn't, and then I swiftly mop it up with my shirtsleeve. That dealt with, I return to my mission. I grab my dad's arm and shake it. 'Wakey wakey, rise and shine!' Nothing. It occurs to me he might be pretending to sleep, waiting to make me jump when I least expect it. But something about his face tells me that's probably not the case. I do the biting thing we do when I'm pretending I'm a wolf and I'm gnawing on his elbow. I bite him really rather hard. And then harder. So hard it makes my teeth hurt a bit. But that doesn't rouse him either, and when I let go of his arm it drops like lead, hanging limply over the side of the bed.

Something is wrong. The tightly-coiled-spring inside my chest is still there, but it no longer feels like excitement. I have a desperate need for my dad to be awake right now. I put both hands on his chest and shake him. I shake him harder, with all my strength. I hit his stomach and I punch his arm and I eventually slap his face, but he doesn't move. I try to shout to my mum but nothing comes out. I stand frozen, staring at my dad's lifeless form, listening to his faint snores for what feels like forever. And then my mind finally kicks into action. I race back to the kitchen in a fraction of the time of my ascent, taking the stairs two at a time even though Mum says it's dangerous. I tell Mum that Dad simply won't wake up. He just won't wake up. Though she dismisses me at first, telling me I better make him wake up if I want to go to the park because she certainly won't be walking me all the way there in her state, she finally comprehends what it is I'm telling her, takes my panic seriously, and pushes past me, running up the stairs as best she can with her protruding stomach. I follow her but can't keep up. When I get to the room I find her crying, screaming, staring at an empty pill bottle on the bookshelf, not far from where I laid the tea.

Things become broken in my memory after that. I can see the ambulance arriving, and I hear myself pleading to be allowed to travel in it with my parents. Funnily enough, I can't recall whether I got my way, and it's never occurred to me to ask, which isn't too strange given I've hardly spoken to anyone about any aspect of that day since. Where did I go if I didn't travel in the ambulance? I remember staying with my aunt for days afterwards, maybe weeks, and crying and crying and crying as she and my uncle tried to pretend everything was fine. But it wasn't fine, I would tell them, because my daddy's in the hospital, he's sick. I don't think I could've known what had transpired that day, I was only four after all. I just knew it was bad.

But at some point I suppose my maturing brain filled in the gaps. I eventually realised my dad had done this to himself. He had wanted to leave this world, a world containing me, my mum, my soon-to-be brother, and eventually, my sister too. And if it weren't for me, he may well have succeeded.

I don't know how to feel about that.

A HYPOTHESIS

Thirty-one years later and I'm watching breakfast news. They're covering a story about a man who killed himself in Newcastle yesterday morning. He burned himself to death in his outhouse. He woke up, doused the building and himself in petrol, and set himself alight. He left his seven-year-old twin girls sleeping in their room, but he attempted to take his wife and ten-year-old son with him. Covered in petrol, he fetched them from where they'd been watching television in the house, dragged them across the garden into the deathbed he'd made, and tried to make them lie in it with him. Luckily his wife was able to escape with the boy, although not without serious burns and damage to the child's lungs.

Discussing this news item on the BBC breakfast sofa is a spokesperson for an anti-suicide charity. He is particularly worried about male suicides. He tells us that of the 5,965 people who killed themselves in the UK last year, 4,508 were men. He wants something to be done. Increase funding, increase awareness, start a conversation. He's very passionate, this campaigner; men are dying. He has a serious slim face and a solemn voice and he's dedicating his life to something he feels is a noble cause. Very commendable. Only I can't help but think the charity has picked the wrong case to use as a platform for their message. The suicide victim in question attempted to burn his wife and ten-year-old son to death. Surely only suicide bombers and Americans who shoot up schools before topping themselves would be less sympathetic?

As I eat my porridge I wonder what would happen if the BBC applied its *balance* rules more evenly. When research conducted by reputable scientists provides further evidence of the irreparable damage we're doing to the planet, the BBC has previously insisted on wheeling in a morally-defunct industry puppet to spew harmful oppositional nonsense in the name of balance. When we had a hugely complex decision to make on whether to stay in the EU or go it alone, the BBC scoured lists of economists to find someone espousing the minority view (amongst economists, at least) that it was a good idea, to ensure we heard both sides. But for this story the campaigner is the only guest, which in itself is fine, but neither of the hosts is even giving him a hard time or playing devil's advocate. They simply nod along.

Of course, there wouldn't be many people falling over themselves to oppose an anti-suicide charity live on national television. But there might be a few. Maybe a representative from a pro-euthanasia group? After all, psychological as well as physical diseases have been accepted in Swiss assisted-suicide clinics. Or someone from a domestic abuse charity, or from the wife's family, neither of whom may have saving such a man at the top of their list of priorities. Or perhaps a spokesperson from a violence-prevention charity or a feminist group, who might care to point out that men also kill *other* people at far higher rates than women do, and so perhaps we should focus on that particular killing problem first.

And if the BBC were getting really creative they could even have invited me, or someone like me. An expert in suicide, albeit in my case suicide in a very specific variety of arachnid. I would never have accepted. I hate publicity almost as much as I hate being filmed, and I have no desire to invite any more threats of violence than are strictly necessary into my life. But in the BBC breakfast sofa fantasy playing out in my head, as I sit on my own sofa in my far-too-juvenile-for-a-thirty-five-year-old koala pyjamas – Jamie bought them for me, so I still wear them even though they're well past their best, and even though my sister Freya calls me *mutton dressed as a geeky toddler* whenever she sees them – with a bowl of porridge balanced on a tray on my knees, I see that I could have been the voice of reason. I, Dr Jessica Miller, could have shared what we already know about suicide: that in nature, it's not always something we consider to be a problem, that it might even be considered sensible, altruistic, adaptive.

If anyone wanted to listen I could tell them that the female Australian redback spider, *Latrodectus hasselti,* likes to eat her male partner during sex. It's kind of her thing. Understandably not all guy spiders are into this particular kink, but the ones that are get to have sex for longer, and so end up fertilizing more eggs and making more baby spiders. The suicidal guy spiders may seem crazy to us. But to nature they make perfect sense. They don't survive their night of passion, so they won't get any other chances to pass on their genes, but that doesn't matter, because they'll have created a crapload of babies who can grow up and do it for them.

Then I'd wow the audience with tales of the self-sacrificial *defender* snapping shrimp of the *Alpheidae* family and naked mole rats, *Heterocephalus glaber,* who choose not to breed, but instead throw themselves into harm's way in order to protect those of their colony who do. Or the humble bumblebee, *Bombus lucorum.* Everyone's favourite insect. There are little flies that like to use the poor bees as a home for their larvae. Once the larvae are inserted into a bee's abdomen, they have only about twelve days to live. But what do the infected bees do? Do they make the most of their remaining time on earth by partying in the colony with their chums? No. Sensing their fate, they actually fly far away and spend their final days alone, presumably to prevent their kin from facing the exact same fate. Although I've always thought this a dubious example of *suicide,* given the infected bee was done for anyway, I'd still mention it to the presenters – who would of course no doubt be hanging on my every word – because the evolutionary psychology literature includes it. More appropriately though, I'd mention the guard honeybee, *Apis mellifera*, that will sting suspected predators to protect the eggs and breeding bees within its hive, even though the guard will pay for said sting with its life. I'd even throw in a plant, *Tachigali versicolor*, a *suicide tree* that flowers only once, before dying in order to create the break in the forest canopy its progeny will need to catch sunlight, survive, and thrive.

And I'd save the best until last. Or not the best really, just mine: *Atypena lentili*, one rather interesting variety of the many money spiders I study. In the 1980s it was noted some of the older female spiders can become barren and yet continue to live for some time afterwards. This in itself was, and still is, quite something given humans and killer whales are among the very few other animals known to undergo something like the menopause. As far as we know, in nature, most other animals remain capable of reproduction until they die. What makes this spider even more interesting is the fact that some of these post-menopausal females then kill themselves. And it's not pretty. They eat their own legs, and presumably then starve and 'bleed' to death.

At this point I should share that evolutionary psychologists and evolutionary biologists – and I say this as an evolutionary psychobiologist – are storytellers. We're fantasists. Everything we conclude is made up. We observe things, and hopefully the observations themselves are not made up. But the inferences we make are. Of course they are. How on earth can we ever know exactly *why* animals do the things they do? How can anyone really *know* that women subconsciously paint their lips red to make them look like aroused vulvas? And indeed, do people even like bright red vulvas? The evidence seems to suggest no. How can anyone ever *know* that heterosexual men are attracted to breasts because they look a bit like bums? And again, do they really look that much like bums? And how can we ever *know* if humans developed creativity, humour, philosophy, in order to have more sex, and therefore more offspring? We can't. We see the *what* and we invent the *why*. And as new observations come in, we *hope* the new stories we invent might get closer to the truth. But they're still stories. I'm not saying we do it deliberately, but when we attribute meaning to an observation, we can only work with what we already know and have experienced. Inevitably our *findings* will more often than not uphold the status quo, or more correctly, our own beliefs.

So when this auto-cannibalistic little critter was discovered, the male scientists involved decided, perhaps you might argue naturally, that the reason for their suicidal behaviour was that the older females recognised they no longer had a use, a function, a meaning. They were old and ugly and past it and barren, no male spider would ever look at them in *that way* again, so why not just eat off all of their own legs? Makes total sense.

Except there's more to the story. After university I joined the group that twenty years previously had discovered this spider's strange behaviour. Although my work was largely focused on a scorpion species at the time, I found myself becoming deeply fascinated by this special money spider. And only partly because the scorpions and larger spiders in the lab scared the absolute crap out of me. I convinced my supervisor to let me build a few chapters centered around *Atypena lentili* into my PhD thesis, and I watched them. I watched and I watched. And I found that not all old and barren *Atypena lentili* females kill themselves. In fact, only a particular type do. That type is the female located close to its female kin, which in nature may not occur frequently, but in the lab often does, *and* still receiving male attention. Only in these cases does the spider get hungry for its own legs. If no other females are present, she lets the males waste their time trying to fertilise non-existent eggs and carries on living. If she's surrounded by kin, but the male spiders are ignoring her in favour of those kin, she hangs around to watch. But if she thinks she's getting in the way of her genes being passed on, getting in the way not by being an old hag, but an irresistible old hottie, she does herself in. Evolutionarily, this makes far more sense than the arguably ageist and sexist initial interpretation. Rather than thinking life is pointless without a man, the older female's sacrifice actively increases the chances of passing on genes she shares.

I'd tell the BBC breakfast audience all of that, probably far overrunning my allotted time, but I'd be on a roll. And so, I'd go on to say, many evolutionary psychologists, including those within my own research group, think of suicide as an inevitable side-effect of being a selfless person, a price we pay for being extremely social animals. We are selfless and social animals not because a supreme being made us in its warm-hearted image, but fundamentally because being selfless and social optimises our chances of passing on our own genes. It makes people want to bed us, for a start. But more importantly, our instinct to protect our family is really an instinct to protect those genes we share with them. And this instinct can be taken further than the family for society's gain. We give blood, we give money, we give time, we become soldiers, police officers, firefighters, ultimately for the sake of our genes. But scientists posit that the same genetic programming that allows our members to dress up in uniform and run into burning buildings to save others, short circuits sometimes. It goes too far. That when people mistakenly miscalculate the value of their life versus their death, so that they feel their death would be more valuable than their life to others around them, especially their family, in passing on their shared genes, then they are pushed, tragically, to kill themselves. There are of course other theories for the evolution of suicide knocking about, but according to this one, erroneous, miscalculated altruism is at the core of most suicides. Taking this to its harsh yet logical conclusion: if we want a human society that contains altruism, then at least for the moment we may have to accept suicide as an unintended dire consequence. It's the rough that comes with the smooth. I'd tell the BBC audience all of this, whether they liked it or not, because it's a widely shared hypothesis within the scientific community.

But that's where I'd stop, for the rest of the truth, or the truth as I see it, may be even less palatable than what preceded it. Because this *evolutionary short circuit* theory isn't one I fully subscribe to. Of course there will always be miscalculations and mistakes. It's a complicated business, measuring one's own worth. And one might suppose depressed people aren't in the best position to do that kind of calculation. But, of course, such a supposition isn't always based on the data. Some studies have shown that depressed people actually assess themselves far more accurately than the mentally healthy. Their ratings of their own intelligence, attractiveness, and popularity in relation to others are more often right than the self-ratings of those in their *right* mind. We might more correctly term mentally healthy people, *healthily deluded*, because they rate themselves as more relatively attractive, intelligent, and popular than they actually are. They overvalue themselves, and so of course they think they better stick around. What would the world do without a gorgeous genius like them? Like us?

So yes, miscalculations and mistakes are inevitable. But I have long hypothesised that the majority of suicides are no evolutionary mishap. Just like the masochistic redback spider males, the stinging bees, and the legless old money spiders, perhaps they're the result of an evolutionarily beneficial trait acting precisely as it should. Aside from the homicidal element of course, perhaps the BBC's tragic arsonist got his sums perfectly right. Perhaps his family will be far better off without him. His wife may remarry and have more children. And more importantly, evolutionarily speaking, with their murderous pyromaniac father gone, perhaps the young daughters and son will now reach adulthood and be well-adjusted enough to have children of their own. The father may be gone, but his genes will live on.

Again, even in my own BBC breakfast fantasy I don't say any of this of course. I've never said any of it to anyone. Not really. I'm alone in these thoughts, alone in my field. Every one of my colleagues took up the study of suicide with the aim of eventually contributing to its prevention. I've come to realise I entered into it with the aim of contributing to its defence.

A SIN

Although not necessarily apologetic, I don't feel altogether comfortable about my stance on suicide. It actually kind of plagues me. More so now, of course. But it always has, and that's been a consistent source of annoyance for me. After all, why should I feel guilty about formulating a sound scientific theory? And not just any theory, but one promising to reassure the world everything is A-ok, hunky dory, just-as-nature-intended? We can probably attribute said discomfort with anything approaching even a neutral view of suicide to the society in which I was raised. Specifically, I'm throwing a lot of the blame towards Saint Augustine of Numidia.

I'm sure you know of good old Saint Gus? Christian scholar, influential philosopher, Bishop of Hippo Regius, born 13th November 354, died 28th August 430? Don't worry if you haven't heard of him, I didn't know much about him either. But once you start looking into suicide at even the most superficial level, his name crops up. It turns out Augustine was a big thinker, and his thoughts have affected the way we in the West live. He came up with the concept of *just wars* being ok, although he felt, generally speaking, we should all be pacifists. I think I'm on board with that. He wasn't into harming Jews and he thought having slaves was a sin. I totally agree with him on both counts, and it's a shame he wasn't more consistently influential in those areas. He had some nice enough stuff to say about women too. Well, nice for the times. Like, 'be kind to your wife, God thinks she's worth it' kind of thing. So that's swell. He wasn't into astrology, which seems smart. And he was a believer in free will and man's overall leaning towards good, which is a nice sentiment at least.

But no one can be right about everything, I guess. Augustine had a bit of a preoccupation with penises and what makes them stand to attention. I'm no historian and certainly no theologian, so I shan't expand – pardon the pun – on the point too much, but from what I can gather, he was convinced Eve eating that fateful apple resulted in him not having perfect control of his member. Instead, along with every other member and vagina out there, it was under evil's spell. Wild. Augustine also chatted divisively about the specific mechanics of the Holy Spirit a lot; like, arguing over whether the spirit came from God, or from God *and* Jesus. Which, although I'm not religious, seems to me to be missing the overall point somewhat. But Augustine is relevant in whatever it is I'm putting together here because of his thoughts on suicide. He came down pretty hard on it. He felt the commandment, *thou shalt not kill* referred to all human life, including one's own. So suicide was a sin, and a big one. It was murder. He was backed up hundreds of years later by Saint Thomas Aquinas (1225-1274) who went so far as to say it was a sin one could never repent from. Bit much. Anyone who attempted suicide was excommunicated from the church if they failed, and if they succeeded they were denied a Christian burial, and their belongings and those of their family could be confiscated. Talk about kicking folks when they're down.

And where the church went, the law dutifully followed. In England and Wales suicide was against the law from the 13th century right up until 1961, and the law only changed in Ireland in 1993. People could actually face criminal prosecution for trying and failing to top themselves, and there are plenty of stories of those who did. That of Lionel Henry Churchill is a particularly striking one. He shot himself in the head while mourning his wife's death, but failed to finish the job. So he was thrown in prison for six months. Neat. People were commonly fined or imprisoned for short stints this way, until politicians like Sir Kenneth Robinson, MP for St Pancras North, and Sir Charles Fletcher-Cooke, MP for Darwen, pushed for a change in the law. They didn't find it easy though. They'd both been plugging away at it for years before the bill was finally passed in 1961, and even then, Prime Minister Harold MacMillan was against it.

So, on the whole, suicide has had a fairly bad rap in my culture. And not just mine. In fact, there are countries in which suicide is still illegal, such as Malaysia, Nigeria, and Lebanon. A translation of Lebanese law I've found online reads: If the person does not commit suicide but attempts to do so, then the penalty shall be imprisonment from three months to two years, and up to three years if it results in a permanent disability or harm. Harsh. Although we're not Lebanese, that's not a world away from some of my older relative's stance on the matter. In their minds, if not punishable, suicide is certainly something to be shameful, hush hush, don't-tell-the-neighbours about.

And even though it's totally and utterly legal now in Britain, we still can't get anyone to *help* us kill ourselves if we're physically unable to, even if that *help* simply means passing us a syringe from a cupboard we can no longer reach. And we still often say *committed* suicide. Like we say *committed* burglary or *committed* assault. Suicide is still a terribly taboo thing one *commits*.

But it doesn't have to be this way, and indeed it's not this way in all cultures. The Japanese are traditionally far more accepting of suicide, with wartime or combat suicides in the form of kamikaze or seppuku historically considered, though of course not by all, to be admirable. Even now, suicide is still regarded by some as the honourable route for those who may bring shame or misfortune to their family, society or country. Don't get me wrong, I think Japan has a bit of a suicide problem, and its government thinks so too and is trying to do something about it. Over twenty thousand Japanese citizens killed themselves last year, and a lot of those suicides were thought to be the result of unemployment and debts. That's a lot of death, and for some pretty horrible reasons. But my point is that as a society the Japanese seem to be leaning more towards my way of seeing things. That the calculation of the worth of one's own life, the consideration of the pros and cons for one's loved ones of sticking around, is maybe a natural and sensible thing to do.

So, if I'm not the first person to wonder if suicide isn't always so bad, why am I struggling with these thoughts?

A BLACK DAY

I've made all the plans.

I hate making plans. But I've done it. I've been on the phone more over these past two weeks than the preceding two years. Someone is forever calling me. There's so much to think about. I'm using a spreadsheet saved in a dedicated folder on my computer. It's the first non-work spreadsheet I've ever made.

There are lots of moving parts. Lots of big and small cogs. Lots of forms to fill in. Lots of bills to pay. Lots of interested parties. Lots of people to inform. Lots of people to listen to. Lots of people who want to listen. Lots of opinions. Lots of contributions. Lots of people who care. Lots of people who feel. Lots of people who understand and who want me to know they understand.

I've been able to step out of it, in a way, by being the coordinator, by thinking about the cogs, the forms, the people, the opinions, the care. I've been able to do this for others.

But now the day is here, and I can't believe what we're all about to do.

A RECURRING THEME

I didn't always want to be a suicide researcher. Obviously. And I certainly had no childhood dreams of working with spiders. Even after all these years they still give me the bloody creeps. When I chose to study biology I did so because I enjoyed the subject. I didn't know whom or what I wanted to be, other than someone with a degree who no longer lives at home. But in addition to my early experiences with my father's failed suicide attempt, three things happened during my study that influenced my direction. I've already told you the first – I learned about suicidal post-menopausal spiders from the very man who discovered them. There's no denying that was pretty cool. But it would've only fleetingly held my interest if two other things hadn't occurred. Here's the first:

I'm nineteen and in my second year of university. I'm living in a tall thin house in Hammersmith with four people I quite like, a few of whom will go on to be some of my closest and longest-standing friends. The one I like best of all is Adam, who sleeps in the attic room above mine. He's the one person at university I actively *decided* to be friends with. When I arrived in my first year I hadn't considered what I would do about friends. On top of being naturally shy and cautious around new people, I also pretty much entirely lack the ability to plan ahead and look forward to things. I've always put this down to the fact that people in survival mode see only the present and very near future, and survival mode was how I'd spent most of my life up until that point. I also missed the small close-knit group I'd been a part of at school, and I couldn't imagine ever finding anyone to replace them. Plus I missed my little sister Freya like crazy. She was only eight at the time, and as weird as it sounds, she was one of my best friends, which perhaps reveals a little something about my maturity levels.

Freya was a huge source of joy in my life, and I felt guilty about leaving her and my brother behind to deal with everything at home while I made a break for freedom. So I was genuinely surprised and somewhat suspicious when smiling strangers would speak to me everywhere on campus, in queues, in lecture halls, in libraries. People who *wanted* to make new friends. I couldn't work out their game. I would second-guess what they were after, because simply wanting to know me seemed quite unbelievable. Of course now I'm glad they spoke to me, and even gladder that some *kept on* speaking to me despite what must've been initially a somewhat frosty reception.

But Adam is different. I first see Adam at a Freshers party in the union, and he stands out amid the sea of posh boys. He doesn't have puffy hair, boating shoes, or a turned-up polo-shirt collar. Or, even worse, the Autumn flipflops, ripped dirty jeans, and tattered string bracelets that are the conspicuous remnants of a gap year. He looks like my friends from home. He's wearing a Smiths t-shirt and converse trainers, and his black hair is a length and style that perfectly, eloquently says *I'm-into-grunge-music-and-I-play-guitar-and-I-have-a-sensitive-side-if-you-care-to-look…but-perhaps-unusually-I-also-wash-my-hair-every-day.*

He's sat in a group, but he isn't looking at or talking to anyone. He seems shy, brooding, and mysterious, like he needs looking after, but at the same time he doesn't need anything or anyone at all, and that is utterly magnetic to me. I deliberately cross the room and speak to him. He is probably the only stranger I ever actively initiate a conversation with at university. And beyond university for that matter. I do it because

I am determined that we will be friends. I will make him my friend, whatever it takes.

Here I will pause, because I recognise I've described Adam as some kind of teen-dream heart throb, so I should probably also make clear that I wasn't motivated by my loins. Perhaps I should've mentioned this by now, but it's always so difficult to know when and how to tell people, and it's especially tricky when you don't currently have a partner you can throw into the conversation, and I'm not sure what I'm even writing anyway or who this is for and so I wasn't sure if you might already know or if it would even be relevant, but, well, I'm a lesbian. Big time. The sort of through-and-through lesbian who's known about their gayness for as long as they can remember. I came out to most of my friends when I was sixteen, and by eighteen, when I met Adam, I'd already had a meaningful relationship with a woman. So when I say I wanted to be friends with Adam, I really mean friends. He looked cool and shy and sensitive and sweet and funny, and I wanted to talk to him.

Back at the Freshers party, I work up a spot of rare social courage – assisted by snakebite and black, which I have only just discovered and find repulsive – and I head over to initiate contact with this stranger, who I tell myself is simply a friend I haven't yet met.

At first Adam gives me the same suspicious look I've recently given everyone else, which of course only makes me like him more. But he soon warms up. And although it turns out he is indeed a posh boy from a private school, apparently difficult to avoid at this university, he is also even funnier and nicer and sweeter and shyer than I had anticipated. So we start hanging out regularly. At some point a group forms around us, people who also want to hang out with us, probably with Adam more than with me. But no matter how large the group grows, Adam and I retain a special bond. When everyone else has gone to sleep, it is he and I who stay up all night making ridiculous short films we're certain are hilarious, but oddly enough no one else seems to understand. It is he and I who regularly take a 4am McDonald's detour after a party, and share secrets over the grey meat and plastic cheese – he about his heartbreaks and unrequited love, me about my home life. And it is he and I who decide early on to live together in the second year, and then some of our friends join us.

By the Easter holidays of that second year, living together has been a roaring success, with all the fun of halls, but in a home that is ours, and that has brought us closer together. Sharing is the currency of friendship, perhaps everywhere, but especially at university. People self-consciously tell stories of their 'weird' families and their tough lives, and bonds form over the exchange. I share just as everyone else does. But I suppose because my stories are worse than everyone else's, people think I've somehow given more, which is possibly why they seem to feel close to me long before I feel close to them. Be that as it may, my housemates and I have by now formed a clear friendship group, and I am growing to love them.

So. Here I am. I'm nineteen and settled in a tall, thin house in Hammersmith, surrounded by people I quite like, possibly love, some of whom I will go on to love and value very much. It's a safe and stable house, the kind where you can make plans and the plans generally happen without any harm coming to anyone. A nice place to be, but especially if you're not used to such places. So especially for me. I've just woken up in that house. It's the second day of the Easter break, but I haven't gone home yet. I don't tend to go home over the holidays unless I have to, and as my family live in London I'll probably just head back for Easter day itself, and maybe nip back to take Freya out for the day a couple of times. Minimise the damage.

Harriet and Adam also haven't gone home yet because today we're heading to a music store on Oxford Street to see one of our favourite bands perform, and get some merch signed. I've bought one of the band's ultra-limited-print records especially for the occasion, despite having never owned or operated or actually even seen a real-life record player. I'll have the vinyl framed once it's signed. Some years later the lead singer will be revealed as a manipulative sicko who preyed on underage girls, causing me to throw the record and the cheap frame away, and to feel physically sick if I ever try to listen to his music. But right now I can't think of a more perfect way to spend a day, and I realise I can't think of anyone I'd rather spend it with than Adam and Harriet. I've had plenty of booze and drug-filled fun over the past year and a half, but it's only at this point that I'm starting to become content at university, to become settled.

I clear the sleep from my eyes and head downstairs to the kitchen where I find Harriet drinking coffee and watching a Peep Show DVD on the tiny television in the corner. I make myself toast and tea and join her at the kitchen table. Harriet and I half watch Peep Show together while we spend a great deal of time screeching our excitement for the gig and signing, and bemoaning how completely un-excited we are for the exams awaiting us after the holidays. Harriet and I can be pretty screechy when we're together, which is surprising to both of us. I'm surprised that this jolly-hockey-sticks rowing-jersey-wearing bleached-blonde-big-haired posh girl is into the same bands as I am. And she's surprised she can have such fun screeching and painting her nails with an emo-goth, lesbian prole.

As we watch back-to-back Peep Show episodes, Harriet flits between discussing her recent breakup, about which she is heartbroken, and the new boy David she's just started seeing, to whom she's very attracted but can't fathom why. Harriet goes on to marry David, but of course I don't know this right then, and having never met him, I assume he's just the rebound guy. We chat for so long it becomes lunchtime, and we make our favourite end-of-the-term-student-loan-instalment meal of chicken super noodles and tinned sweetcorn. We ponder what to wear to the gig while we eat, and then both head upstairs to get washed and changed into the edgy-yet-casual outfits we've selected. Our rooms are next door to one another, so we share regular updates while we dress, and play the band's music, each blaring different songs competitively.

When it comes time to leave, I'm running predictably late. Harriet moans at me, but only in jest. She's used to it by now, and if tardiness truly bothered her I very much doubt she would ever have entered into a friendship with me. I'm reassured by the fact Adam hasn't appeared from his room yet – he's often even later than I am – so I obviously still have time to do the quiff hair thing Harriet taught me recently. I've pretty much mastered the style now, however under time pressure I fumble, and fumble I do today. Harriet is watching, which isn't helping, so I tell her to go and pester Adam instead of breathing down my neck, as he's bound to take some corralling. I can see she's torn between the joy of making further fun of my huge butter fingers – 'fat-handed twat' is a favourite jibe – and the logic of speeding Adam up. The angel shoulder wins, and she heads up to Adam's room.

She's not gone for long though, and when she returns she looks annoyed. Adam's not there. Is she sure? He's a big guy, it's a small room, she's sure. She scours everywhere else in the house and reports back that he's nowhere to be found. We check our phones and there's been no word. Harriet is turning from annoyed to angry. She's ok with tardiness, but she cannot abide this kind of inconsiderate behaviour. Has he popped out? Has he gone ahead? How are we to know if he doesn't bother to message us? I don't feel annoyed, I feel concerned. I realise I didn't see Adam last night. I ask Harriet if she saw him, and she says no. Upon recalling that fact she now feels certain he's got lucky, maybe with that Physics girl he's liked for a while. Or perhaps the Chemistry one who obviously fancies him. I force myself to feel some relief at this explanation. Adam's a popular guy, so it seems plausible, and this wouldn't be the first time he's stayed out all night without letting anyone know. He's also a live-in-the-moment person, which makes him engaging company, but not too great at texting. What better moment to live in than a hook-up, I guess? But we can't leave without Adam, can we? Harriet tells me we can. In fact, she's convinced that right now he's heading to the gig from wherever it was he slept. So, we both text him as well as leave him a note just in case he decides to swing by here first, and then head out ourselves.

I shouldn't really say this in light of the lead singer's one-day-to-be-revealed heinous crimes, but the gig is epic. The best I've ever seen them. And because it's an in-store it's astoundingly intimate, and we're able to get so close we can see the spit flying out of the screamo singer's mouth. Maybe if they weren't so damn entertaining, or so very charming while signing our merchandise, and maybe if I didn't have the biggest crush on the lesbian bassist, I would have thought of Adam more. But it only occurs to me we haven't run into him as we leave the store.

We text Adam to say we're heading to Garlic n' Shots, a goth pub I love, and will still love even many years later, and that Harriet surprisingly loves too, despite her standing out like a sore thumb. We take up residence in one of the underground alcoves, and with no phone signal and garlic-y shots inside us, forget all about Adam for a few hours. When we return to street-level upon leaving and no news comes in from him, we record a grainy phone video of the two of us singing, loudly and badly, one of the paedo-band's songs, and send it to him.

We're on a high; the weather's just starting to get a little warmer and tomorrow Harriet will go *home home* and we'll both start to take revision seriously. So tonight we will revel in our youth and our freedom. We grab a shish kebab at the rather delicious all-night takeaway nearby, making conversation with other drunk patrons as we wait for our order. We catch the bus and sing with our mouths full of chilli and garlic the entire journey home. We are exactly the kind of people with whom you'd hate to share a bus, and we're loving it. When we arrive home, where Adam is not, we crank up the music and sit in the kitchen smoking weed out of the open door. We speak until our mouths ache. I won't remember what we speak about, but I'll be certain it was deep. We're both terribly deep.

At some point it's decided Harriet's new fling David will come over after his night out, and I'm excited to meet him. He saunters in all floppy haired and plum mouthed, but I can tell he's nervous to meet me and trying to impress Harriet's friend, so I like him immediately. Just as well. We chat and laugh for ages until I realise – embarrassingly late – that I'm a third wheel who's outstayed her welcome, so I retire to bed as the sun is rising.

The last thing I do before I sleep is text Adam to tell him about the amazing day I've had. I'm sad he's missed it, but it couldn't have been more perfect, I tell him. It seems highly likely the bassist and I will fall in love. Harriet's new beau is a public schoolboy rugger bugger tool, but I like him. We should always live together, forever. Promise? I'm drunk and high and exhausted and happy. I ask him where he is purely out of interest, not concern. Then I sleep.

Beeping and buzzing wake me. My head hurts and my mouth feels like a lizard died violently inside it a year ago. Why have I set my alarm? Why would I do something stupid like that? Bright sunlight is shining through my low-quality blinds. I came home one evening last month and I saw from the street that someone was in my room. Adam was retrieving a CD I'd forgotten to return to him. From outside I could see everything, every detail, the disappointed look on his face as he found the CD in the wrong case, the care he took as he returned it to its rightful home. I wondered why he'd opened my blinds, as I rarely bothered to. And then I realised he hadn't. They were 'closed'. That's how bad those blinds were, and I'd been undressing in front of them for six months. I'd even taken a date back there once. Mortifying. But not mortifying enough for me to do anything about it. I simply change my clothes in the bathroom now and have determined that if I'm ever lucky enough to engage in coitus again, I'll go to their place. So the sunlight shining through these useless blinds is letting me know it's the middle of the day, and that this appalling noise is no alarm, it must be a call.

I reach down and grope around the floor where I've left my phone. I find it and see 'Adam Home' calling. He must've gone home already without telling us. Strange. I pick up and tell him in a croaky but mock-forceful voice how much trouble he's going to be in with Harriet. This unpredictable bullshit may work on some ladies, but not her.

But it's not Adam. It's his mum. My surprise at hearing her voice initially masks something alarming. She's crying. When that finally registers I sit bolt upright in bed, suddenly wide awake, my heart pounding, my alcohol-raw stomach churning. She's trying to say something but I can't understand, and I feel disrespectful as I loudly ask her to please slow down. Then Adam's father takes the phone, and as he does I hear him saying he knew he should've been the one to do this.

He tells me they're calling because Adam mentioned me a lot. He says he hopes I can pass on news to anyone I think should know. Two days ago Adam committed suicide. He jumped in front of a train. He says there will be a funeral in time, after the police have finished what they need to do, and he hopes I will make it along. He says there isn't much he can say right now, he doesn't know what to say, but they decided people should know, that we might be worried. I suppose we were worried, but it was a far nicer feeling than this. I don't say that. I thank him, tell him I'm sorry, so, so, sorry. His voice breaks as he says goodbye.

I knock on the wall between my and Harriet's bedroom hard and repeatedly before I realise she's probably left. I vaguely remember drifting in and out of sleep as her parents were picking her up this morning. I spend the rest of the day crying and vomiting, vomiting and crying. In between trips to the bathroom I manage to contact everyone I can think of who knew Adam, which only makes the crying and vomiting worse. I do not start my serious revision schedule as planned.

Three weeks later and I arrive at the funeral in Coventry late. I'm relieved to find it hasn't started. I have yet to learn weddings and funerals always begin a bit later than billed, giving the star of the show plenty of time to have their makeup done. I quietly add myself to a row of university friends from Adam's first-year halls, next to Harriet. We don't have time to talk because the ceremony kicks off as I sit. Sombre classical music starts up, but it's rather tinny and distant. An unseen hand cranks up the volume, but too vigorously, causing aggressively loud violins and ferocious feedback to fill the air. They respond rapidly but overcompensate so the music becomes inaudible. This fiddling continues for a few more moments, during which I wonder how many people who are pretending not to notice what is so obviously unavoidably noticeable are also trying not to laugh. I know if Adam were standing next to me we wouldn't have been able to contain our giggles. The thought chokes me, helpfully erasing any humour. There is a collective sigh of relief when the music finally reaches an acceptable volume and we can proceed.

It's a fairly conventional service, except far shorter than the handful of others I've been to, and not so well attended. At age nineteen I've been to four funerals. Two were for my grandparents, one was for my uncle. The only funeral I've been to for a young person so far took place last year for my school friend's younger sister. She died of cancer aged sixteen. It was a huge affair, the church full of other young people and parents and teachers. The sermon was long and moving, celebrating her short life, while trying to make sense of a world in which a kind, intelligent, funny, beautiful young woman can be cut down before ever reaching her prime. Family and friends queued to add their thoughts, wishes, and readings to the ceremony. Most people were standing as the pews were all taken.

This, my fifth funeral, and my second funeral for a young person, feels a world apart. We're in a crematorium with utilitarian décor and fewer than half the pews are full. The sermon is short, and I can't be the only person who finds it a little awkward. Adam's manner of death is not referred to directly, so it hangs there all the more clearly in our minds. There is no wake, as such. I'm not clear if that reflects a family tradition or the awkward circumstance. But there's tea and coffee being served in the foyer, and half the mourners stick around for a hot drink.

Harriet and I gather with three other friends from university, Nat and Anthony, our other housemates, and Kelly who was my neighbour in halls and used to have a crush on Adam. We're avoiding silence and serious thought by talking about the usual things no one cares but everyone talks about: our journeys to the crematorium, the weather, how the tea is quite nice, how we're planning on getting home. But Adam's mother has other ideas. She approaches our group and thanks us for attending. And then one by one she looks us in the eyes and she's crying while she asks us each individually why Adam did it and what she could have done to stop him.

We're full of guilt and grief as we each have to tell her in turn that we don't know. Behind her Adam's father, two younger sisters, and his half-brother and sister from his father's first marriage look on helplessly. It's the saddest thing any of us has witnessed first-hand, a mother flailing, begging for answers she hopes will heal her incurably broken heart.

Eventually answers come, but not of the healing variety. Two weeks after the funeral I arrive at university for a lecture and my friends are behaving strangely. They've been treating me like damaged goods ever since Adam died. I don't blame them. I either make them afraid of catching my misery, or guilty about not feeling more miserable themselves. But today their weirdness is heightened, their silence pregnant rather than inept. Eventually someone hands me a newspaper and points to an article. It seems the press have got wind of Adam's story. I'm annoyed at not having found the article myself. I've been using all my energy to focus on the once small but suddenly huge steps necessary to live my life – brushing teeth, washing hair, remembering to eat, setting alarm clock, renewing bus pass – so catching up on current affairs has fallen by the wayside. But that's no excuse. I nearly missed this.

My heart is pounding in my ears as I read. It feels surreal, to see my own tragedy reported as news. Adam is, was, a real person in my real life, not a character in today's paper. Promising young London student thirtieth to commit suicide since January, reads the headline. From the article I learn Adam had downed a bucketload of pills and alcohol before jumping in front of the train, so he really wanted to get the job done. I learn his father – sixty years-old – was a senior civil servant in the foreign office and owned three homes. I hadn't known what his dad did or how old he was. I would have guessed older. It's strange that this is how I learn things. That whoever wrote this article knows more about my friend than I do. I learn Adam had been struggling in his course and frequently missing lectures. We all missed lectures, especially morning ones. Had Adam been missing more than the rest of us? Evidently he had. I learn he'd had mental health difficulties going back to his early teens. He'd told me he sometimes felt sad and frustrated and wondered what the point of it all was. But we all said tortured teen things like that when we were drunk and trying to be deep. I hadn't taken him seriously enough.

Then I read about Holly. Holly was someone on Adam's course he'd mentioned a few times. He told me he fancied her and that sometimes she seemed to like him back, but at other times she seemed to be leading him on to make others jealous. She sounded like a bit of a bitch to me, although I hadn't given her much thought. From the newspaper I learn that after Holly had rejected his advances, Adam had started harassing and stalking her. He'd inundated her phone, university email, MSN messenger and MySpace account with aggressive, threatening, sexual, perverse messages and images. The papers quote some of them and they make me feel sick. He'd also spread rumours about her amongst their course mates. On a couple of the rare occasions Adam had attended lectures that year, he'd deliberately sat next to or behind Holly, passing hateful notes and whispering spiteful things. I learn Holly had become afraid to go to lectures, so she'd stopped coming into university. But Adam had found out where she lived and worked, and had been making frequent nuisance calls and visits, even staying outside her house all night a couple of times. I learn that the week of Adam's death the university had been informed of the stalking, and that Adam was due to meet the head of his course on the day he'd killed himself, but he never turned up. I learn that this had been going on for months without me noticing. I learn that I'm a gullible, unobservant idiot, a bad judge of character, and a bad friend.

Two weeks later and I feel like a stalker myself. I'm in the physics building where Adam used to have his lectures. I've only been here a couple of times before, but I somehow know exactly where to sit to get a clear view of people as they enter and leave the main lecture theatre without being noticed myself. A bell rings and students pour out of the room. There must have been about a hundred in there, and as the crowd starts to thin I'm giving up hope, but then at the back of the stream I see her. I've found out what she looks like from Google and MySpace, and I now see a girl who is definitely Holly, although she's smaller in person than I'd gathered from the photos. She's hugging a plastic folder of notes to her chest as she laughs with two friends. They stop at the water fountain to fill their bottles, and although I don't know her, as Holly chats to these friends she seems unmistakably happy and easy and free.

Since reading about Holly in the paper I've spoken to a couple of the guys I vaguely know from Adam's course. I was hoping the papers had got their facts wrong, or that Holly was a delusional liar. It could happen, and if it had happened I'd planned to find every copy of that worthless rag and burn it in front of that lying witch Holly's house. But the physics boys confirmed everything I'd read, and more. Holly was not a lying witch. I'd thought those physics guys were Adam's friends, and I suppose they used to be, but they'd distanced themselves from him after he'd started what they described as 'a fucked up creepy campaign of hate' against Holly, which they could see was ruining her life, and sensed would end in violence.

If Adam had carried out the threats he'd made against Holly, she would have become a rape or a murder victim. But even if he hadn't, the threats themselves were enough to have a significant impact on her life. Over the past week I'd researched stalking and the effects the crime has on victims, and I'd learned that many suffer symptoms of post-traumatic stress disorder. People change their lives because of this stuff, changing jobs and cities and names. Holly had stopped going to lectures. Victims can suffer flashbacks, anxiety attacks, and problems with intimacy, trust, and sex. Adam was already committing acts of aggression and terror against Holly, and was threatening to do worse.

Seeing her here, back at university and apparently happy, confirmed what I'd started to think since reading that awful article. That of all the things that could have come out of this fucked up situation, maybe Adam's suicide wasn't the worst. As much as losing him had broken my heart, I was starting to feel glad that the violence he'd committed had been against himself and not someone else. More than that, I was starting to think maybe this was meant to be, maybe it was for the best. Maybe Adam had done his sums, and his evolutionary calculations had been correct. His death would mean that another person, a person for whom in some sick way he clearly cared a lot, could live.

A MEETING

'Ok, so eyes closed people. That means you too Susanne. No cheating. Now everyone hold out your hands and display your marks out of ten.'

This is how we score books in our book group. We do it this way so as not to be influenced by other people's opinions. Then we pick on the high and low scorers and make them speak up first. Although I usually tend to feel a little shy about public speaking, and so opt for a more middling mark than I might otherwise bestow, today I boldly proffer all ten digits. It's the first ten I've given in this group. Maybe one of the only tens I'll ever give. I've told Freya – who boasts she's a member of the group when she wants to impress any guy who seems even remotely cerebral, despite the fact she's failed to attend a single meeting – that if she reads only one book group book ever, this should be the one. She pretended to ignore me, but as I handed her my copy to borrow, I could sense she'd probably give it a go. And she won't be disappointed. In my opinion this author is a bloody genius.

'Ok everyone can open them now.'

I look around and I'm not surprised to be surrounded by a sea of nines and tens. I'm glad I won't be forced to speak up if I don't want to. Then I see the exception: controversial Rachel. She can always be counted on to buck the trend. Rachel's given the book a two, and the two fingers she's chosen to present appear to say as much about her feelings for the book as the score itself.

'Ok let's start with some of the tens, shall we? Anyone want to say why they loved this fantastic book choice so much?'

Ashley is chairing because she picked the book this month. It's not a competition or anything, but you can see from her beaming face that Ashley knows it kind of is a competition, and she's pretty pleased to have suggested such a popular book. As an entirely cis and heterosexual person, Ashley's a minority in our roughly 80% queer membership, and she correctly predicted this big gay book would win over our big gay group.

Sabrina announces she'd be happy to start. As usual. I can see people subtly rolling their eyes. But again, as usual, Sabrina seems oblivious. It's generally a friendly book club, so when some members tend to dominate, some members being Sabrina, no one does anything about it. Sabrina shares how her gay male friend read the book when it first came out and how he thinks it's one of the best and most important gay novels ever written, and Sabrina agrees, but she thinks it also transcends sexuality and is actually about something much more, that it's about good and evil and happiness and suffering, that it's a modern fairy tale, albeit a dark one, that it's a timeless novel she will return to again and again. Nothing to disagree with there. She took the words right out of my mouth, without giving a thought to whether I would like to remove them from my mouth myself via the act of speaking. And, in fairness, she made them far more eloquent and coherent than I ever could.

Then Sabrina tells us of the visceral reactions the book provoked in her. The buckets of tears she shed over the tragedies, the bathtubs of tears she shed over the touching moments. I nod along animatedly, as does everyone else. Apart from, I notice, Rachel. I've been quite the blubber since Jamie and I ended. A tender advertisement love story between a woman and her yoghurt can set me off. But this book was different. These tears weren't confined to the privacy of my own home, and they weren't the sort that could be bravely held back, or even, as is the case for a particularly touching piece of dairy-product marketing, culminate in a single wistful teardrop running down my cheek. No. This book was something else. During commute reads I felt absolutely no shame in pouring emotions onto the strangers crammed against me in a tube carriage, my tears dampening their suit jackets and scarves, and my heaving body shaking them more than the rattling train. During one stint reading while sat on a bus, an episode in the novel had me so thoroughly livid that I threw the book against the chair in front of me. I hurled it with such incensed vigour that it bounced back and onto the lap of the person next to me, to whom I apologized. Which I probably wouldn't have had to do had they read the book, because they would've surely understood the point I must have reached, and remembering it, they would quite rightly have thrown the book on the floor in renewed rage themselves. Which they did not do. The throwing. Therefore they obviously must not have read it yet. So yep, I agree with Sabrina again, and I show this through further nodding, and also by trying to interject with a story of my own emotional reaction. But it appears Lucy, Mo, Shadae, and Clare are all trying to do the same thing concurrently, and so we all falter out of politeness, which leaves enough of a gap for Sabrina to continue.

'Because don't you all think,' Sabrina asks, 'that actually the main character, and I think we can all agree that he was indeed the main character, was sort of like a Jesus character, or at least a kind of Job character, or a saint or something? He was even named for one, after all? And don't you all concur that the evil that befell him was biblical in its proportions? And you must all concede that some of the other main characters, and two in particular, were rather angelic in their virtue? And with all that in mind, we must therefore accept that it was actually a modern-day parable in many ways; a parable about the nourishing nature of friendship, the lifegiving strength of family, the way that love can help one overcome anything? Y'know?'

Sabrina's case is closed. The case presumably being that she's the smartest and best reader in our book club. A case she always wins. A silence is left, which Rory, who also awarded the book full marks, starts to fill. He hadn't been thinking about it that way before, but now that he is, Sabrina's point certainly makes sense to him, and would tally with the lack of significant time-markers, like, say, the 9-11 tragedy, in the book. A parable needs no particular context, and in fact giving a parable context may dilute its message and generalisability.

Olli pipes up in agreement and adds that he liked the focus on the personal, not the wider context. It made the book more claustrophobic, in a good way, and more realistic.

'Ultimately, it is the personal that really matters to us all,' Olli says.

Despite the fact Olli has just agreed with him, Rory irritably disagrees with Olli, saying actually many people, including notably Rory himself, *do* care about politics and the wider world and global events, and although he appreciated the focus on the personal in this particular book, maybe Olli was actually in the minority of *real* people, at least in today's hyper-connected world, who didn't seem to care about anything going on around them.

Olli retorts that this excellent book written by this excellent author, which everyone in this book group loved – he's obviously missed or forgotten Rachel's two out of ten – was evidence Rory's assumption that everyone in the world is like him or should be like him in obsessing over global events that have no direct bearing on his own life, whilst ignoring the things he deems beneath him that actually do impact his own life and the lives of those around him, like say the washing up or organising the big shop delivery, doesn't seem to be quite right.

If it hasn't become obvious to you already, Rory and Olli are a couple. They are both valued members of the book club, and it's my guess they use our monthly meetings as a way to passive-aggressively vent their frustrations with one another. Which strikes me as quite healthy behaviour, given their relationship seems rather strong overall, and they rarely fight or bicker in any other setting. Despite being glad that it's perhaps helping them bond, today their sniping is starting to give me that unbearably awkward feeling like I have an itch inside my stomach I have to reach inside and scratch or I'll explode.

I'm therefore glad when Lucy changes the subject. Lucy is over the moon to have read a book that so clearly centred a non-binary character, because, even though it wasn't mentioned explicitly, of course everyone can agree the main character was non-binary, right? This is Lucy all over. Lucy is non-binary, which I absolutely and completely accept and respect. There are two trans and two other non-binary members of our book group, and I even think if I were ten years younger, as Lucy is, I'd probably call myself non-binary too. The definition fits me now and always has. But using the actual term *non-binary* publicly about myself, or asking people to refer to me as *they* or *zi*, would somehow feel like the identity equivalent of donning tight leather trousers: I'd be mutton dressed as lamb. So no one cares that Lucy is non-binary. Lucy's issue is they're not content with simply being non-binary themselves, they feel the need to claim everyone else is non-binary too. Which is totally understandable really; all queers do it. When the stories you grow up with don't feature anyone like you, you're forced to take literary liberties and see queerness wherever you possibly can. So it wouldn't have to be an issue at all, at a push it could simply be amusing. Except whenever Lucy brings this into book group, things tend to turn ugly. When they suggested Heathcliff was NBi and the group weren't convinced, Lucy screamed at us all for erasing masculinity from non-binary identities and zealously upholding the gender binary in a fashion that would make Kate Bush ashamed. When Lucy pondered if Barbara Covett was perhaps genderqueer, Mo, who is also non-binary, lost their shit, claiming that by attempting to bring a blackmailing sociopath into the NBi fold, Lucy was doing precisely what all Daily Mail-reading bigots do: equating gender divergence with moral deviance. And when Lucy decided Jo March was genderqueer, which we all entertained far more than most of their other suggestions, Sabrina branded us heteronormative misogynists because we couldn't believe a woman could possibly write and be independent and assertive and interesting and still be a *woman*.

Sensibly, no one takes the gender-neutral bait this time, and after a few moments of awkward silence, during which people pretend to privately consider Lucy's suggestion, Ashley moves us on.

'Sabrina, I agree it was fairy tale-like, or biblical.' She says, 'It showed how powerful love and friendship can be. At its core, it was a story of hope. But it was a tragedy too. It was a lesson that you should always carry on, no matter what, because there are people who love you. I now get why my sister named her baby after him. He, the lead character, was so strong, and he coped with so much, and if only he could have carried on a little further, it all would have been ok.'

People chime in with their assent. So wonderful, they all felt, that he overcame so much and strove for happiness and attained it. So sad, they all lament, that he couldn't hang on a little longer. A lesson to us all. We must hang on. It's important and worth it in the end, they're saying.

Up until this point I've been in total agreement with them all, even with the bits that sort of went over my head. This ten-out-of-ten robbed-of-the-Man-Booker novel is a bloody triumph. I've never before cared about characters in a novel so deeply. I've never before felt so grateful to an author for creating happiness, or so angry at an author for creating suffering. But the conversation has started to confuse me, and not in the lofty intellectual way it usually does.

I mean, the book is great, the author is great, the characters will no doubt become iconic. But naming your baby after the monumentally miserable lead? Surely I can't be the only one in the room who thinks that's kind of tempting fate? And more importantly, how can they all think this skilled writer intended us to learn one should suffer on stoically no matter what? How can they believe the message to be life at all costs?

On the contrary, I felt the message was clear: sometimes life is worse than the alternative. I read the themes as being: What is a life worth? And who is a life for? Is hope sometimes pathological? Was the lead character soldiering on for the benefit of others? Is that what we should do? Suffer countless blows and indignities and near-constant mental and physical anguish the way he did, for the sake of others? And, crucially, did his soldiering on actually *help* any of the others? Or were their lives made more miserable by association with his struggle? Were they only truly freed when death was chosen by their loved one? And if that choice – death – had been made earlier, after the initial brutal sadness, how much pain might it have prevented? How much happiness might this one death have allowed to flourish?

But I don't need to say any of this, because this is where Rachel enters the conversation, which is always the best bit of book club for me.

'What a load of bollocks,' she begins.

'Which bit is bollocks precisely?' The rest of the group enquire.

'All of it.' Rachel replies. 'The book, and everything you bunch of jokers just said about the book: all bollocks. If I hadn't been reading it for book group I would've burned it as soon as it became clear the main character was such a limp piece of wank, which was near enough immediately.'

Rachel has a real way with words. Rory tries to respond, but Rachel's on a roll.

'The characters were completely unbelievable, which makes total sense once you realise the author did absolutely zero research on trauma and self-harm and suicide. As if a guy like that could have kept up a ridiculously high-powered city job. As if any of them could reach the levels of success they reached with their ridiculous personalities. Bollocks. And as for the suicide thing – why the fuck didn't he get it over with sooner? It would've been far more realistic, and it would've spared everyone a hell of a lot of pain, especially me because I wouldn't have had to read all of his pathetic self-pitying bullshit. I wanted to give this book a zero because it made me so angry, but in the end I gave it one point because I didn't notice any spelling or grammatical errors, and a second point because at least the character made me happy in the end by doing the right thing and just bloody topping himself. And another thing: your sister should be flipping sectioned for naming her child after that horrifically unlucky numpty.'

That's Rachel. She's only here to keep me company. I dragged her with me when I first joined this new local queer-friendly book group, which I found online after leaving the group Jamie and I had regularly attended together, and over a year later I'm still too shy to come alone. It's nice for me to have her here, and it's nice for the group too, given Rachel's the most valuable member really, as her input always gets everyone chatting heatedly for at least a further hour. Most importantly, today she's reassured me I'm not alone in my thoughts.

When the meeting ends, Rachel and I walk to the station together. She fills me in on the latest women to fill her in. She's been forced to move to a new dating app, having exhausted the last one's supply. I return our conversation to the novel.

'Your comments were great on the book today,' I say, 'So good to hear a dissenting voice to spice the meetings up.'

'Hope it wasn't too strong,' Rachel replies, 'I just found the book so long and so boring and I wanted to stir things up, and I just instinctively want to disagree with anything Sabrina ever says.'

'No, I thought what you said was good. Like, really good.'

'And funny I hope,' Rachel says as we arrive at the station. 'I guess I was just being a bit of a dick, I've had a weird week. I obviously don't believe anything I said in there. Suicide is a terrible tragedy, and never the right option, and blah blah blah, so even I wasn't happy when that stupid boring character I didn't care about offed himself. I was just glad it meant the book was finally going to end, but I guess I shouldn't make light of it in that way. Like, I obviously don't think that's ever a good choice, and now I'm thinking that I hope no one in the group has had any experiences with it, because then I've been a real bitch. Sometimes I can't help myself, though. It's nice to play the monster, y'know?'

'Yeah, I know.' I say, as we hug goodbye and head to our separate platforms. I'm alone again. And now I'm a monster too.

Will you think I'm a monster?

A HUNGER

And then there was Beth. I'm sixteen when I encounter Beth and her girlfriend Jo. They're nineteen and pretty much the coolest people I've ever met, and certainly the first *out* lesbians. I instantly knew they were a couple, because on their first day working in the shoe shop where I have a part-time job, they arrived holding hands and kissing. I spend four weeks working alongside them before I speak to either of them. In week two I notice Jo has that little bit of the ear – the bit that sticks out in front of the ear hole – pierced. I look it up and discover it's called a tragus. I hadn't even registered that tragi – plural of tragus, I imagine – exist, let alone could be pierced. A week later I beg a school friend to accompany me to Camden to get mine done, dragging her from shop to shop until I find an earring that looks exactly like Jo's. Having a needle of not insignificant girth shoved through a chunk of my cartilage is fairly painful, and given my larger-than-average-ears look best with no attention drawn to them whatsoever, the piercing doesn't become me in quite the way it does Jo. But I love it and can't stop looking at myself in the mirror.

Beth has short white-girl dreadlocks that make her look like she's in a band, probably a ska band. I briefly toy with the idea of getting dreadlocks too. I figure its exceptionally frizzy, wiry texture could make my hair a perfect candidate. But I've been burned too many times before, so I accept most things that work with other people's hair will not

44

work with mine, and I refrain, for which future me will be eternally grateful once she learns the term *cultural appropriation*. I settle instead for buying a bandana, a black version of the purple one Beth wears when she leaves work. I also buy a vegan cake, because I have an inkling at least one of my real-life-lesbian colleagues – oh my god I can't believe I get to work alongside real-life-lesbians – is a vegan or vegetarian.

But although I'm now armed with metal in my ear, fabric on my head, and almond butter in my stomach, I have no intention of ever actually speaking to Beth or Jo. The three-year age gap between us feels like a generation. They are edgy grown-ups and I'm a lame school kid waiting for my GCSE results. Simply knowing a Beth and a Jo exist, and exist in my world, is enough to provide hope and inspiration. I expect nothing more. Yet four weeks into their summer stint at the shop, I do speak to Jo. In fact, Jo is the first person to whom I come out as gay. Furthermore, coming out as gay is the first thing I ever say to her. I don't plan it that way, I'm taken by surprise.

It's a Saturday lunchtime and I've just gone to the deli next door and bought an entire full-sized loaf of fresh sun-dried tomato bread, which I'm working my way through, the whole thing, in the shoe shop's staff room. I am not a svelte sixteen-year-old. I recognise this is not normal behaviour so I usually sit somewhere else in the shopping centre to eat my week's-worth-of-bread-in-one-sitting. But today I've been given a late break time, making me even more ravenous, so no one is supposed to be on lunch at the same time as me. I'm halfway through my loaf when Jo storms in, furious.

'A rude teenager just called me a stupid dyke because we don't make the shoes he wants in his tiny-penis shoe size,' she shouts. 'I can't believe Gav, that bloody useless boss of ours, was standing right there when the jumped-up prick said what he said and he did absolutely nothing about it, and I'm just supposed to smile politely and put up with this bigoted fucking bullshit. I wish I'd punched the cocky little twat in his weedy little throat and kicked all his sniggering fucking friends in the balls.'

Jo's not really speaking to me. She's saying all of this to the room, to the unwashed cups, to the grubby chairs, to the tiny window framing only the bricks in the wall of the building a few metres away. But then she turns to look at me, expecting a response, looking red and aggressive, looking like I'm the one she wants to punch in the throat.

'I'm a stupid dyke,' I say without thinking, my mouth still full of greasy sun-dried-tomato-bread.

Jo stands there for a few seconds, taking me in, and then bursts into laughter. 'I'm a stupid dyke too, actually,' she says, 'Stupid for getting so worked up over a fucking idiot kid. So maybe the little prick was simply stating the fucking obvious.' She pauses, stares at me. 'I'm Jo, by the way. Who are you, and are you really a dyke?'

I tell her who I am, and that yes I think I'm a dyke, although currently in thought and not deed. Jo immediately forgets about her anger, and also the fact she should be on the shop floor serving customers. She spends the rest of my lunchtime in the staffroom with me, and by the time my hour is up she's taken me under her wing, a kind of pet newbie lesbian project, and convinced me to join her and Beth at a new gay club called The Ghetto the following Thursday. Jo knows the owner and can ensure my tender age will be no barrier to entry. We swap numbers – I can't believe I have a real life lesbian's number in my phone – and as we head back to the shop floor Jo compliments me on my tragus piercing. I thank her, telling her it's nothing really, I've had it for years.

I refuse the overtime my boss offers for Thursday evening because I have big gay plans. I get hardly any sleep on Wednesday night I'm so excited. I spend all day Thursday trying on outfits and watching the clock. I consider texting Jo to check the dress code, but decide that looks très uncool and desperate, so I dress as close to Jo/Beth-wear as possible: baggy jeans, skate shoes, a tight top, a rope necklace with a cross on it. I worry I look too casual, but when I see Beth approaching as I wait at the station, I realise the tight top was a little dressy. I also realise I've never said one word to Beth. I had assumed they'd arrive together, because they're always together. But here is Beth walking towards me and I'm suddenly ten times more nervous than the already-very-nervous I was a few seconds ago. I blurt out, 'Where's Jo?' before I even say hello, then immediately appreciate how rude I'm being and apologise. This could have been a fairly awful introduction, except Beth's a pool of tranquillity, a calming influence, as peaceful and considered as Jo is brash and loud, so she soon puts me at ease.

'Jo's already in town,' she says, 'she'll meet us at a bar near the club.'

I go on to have a long, drunk, magical night in the club I will visit nearly every week, through my sixth form, university, then PhD years, until it tragically turns off its music and turfs out its lushes for good. I consume countless glasses of cheap luminous red vodka and cranberry, and dance all night long pressed up against the other booze and sugar-fuelled hedonists crammed into the sweaty basement. I have never been happier and felt more at home than in this grubby underground world full of people like me, and I experience genuine and instant love for the girl who takes my entrance money and stamps my hand, the girl who checks my coat and bag, the girls who keep my plastic cups filled, the girls who touch their fingertips to the dripping ceiling as they dance, the girls in the endless queue for the horrible toilets, the girls who don't wait in the queue and instead brave the infinitely more horrible men's toilets. The girls, the girls, the girls.

Spurred on by Beth and Jo, I have my first lesbian kiss with a much older German woman who couldn't be further from my *type* if she had a beard and a penis, and I wonder if the fact I don't really enjoy it means maybe I'm not gay after all – it doesn't. On the long bus ride home, and on many more similar bus rides throughout the summer and for years beyond, as we eat our tasteless but very reasonably priced all-night-pizza slices, which are sometimes actually very tasty kebabs, I get to know my saviours, my mentors, my friends, Beth and Jo.

This is what I learn.

Beth and Jo met in their first year at university. Jo studies Economics, Beth Psychology. They both picked their subjects fundamentally because they want to understand people better. Seems obvious with

Psychology, but I had never thought of Economics that way. Now I can't think of a subject that couldn't be pursued, at its core, out of a desire to understand people better. They both love music even more than I do, and they know so many more cool and obscure bands, and have actually seen them play live rather than just shouting along to CDs in their room. Beth introduces me to folk music, Jo to riot grrrl. I will be forever grateful for this. They have matching tribal tattoos on their ankles, which I regard as the most romantic thing I've ever seen. They plan to, and then they do, go travelling together for six months after they graduate – I miss them terribly during this time – to visit simpler places before joining the rat race. The races they join, and have always wanted to join, are PR (Beth) and a left-leaning think tank (Jo). Beth is quiet and thoughtful and calm. Jo's just as fiery as she first appeared, except when it comes to her interactions with Beth, where I've never seen a more patient gentle soul. They're both lovely with Freya. A true marker of my respect is if I trust someone enough to introduce them to my little sister. They accompany me to playgrounds and kiddie movies with her. Freya thinks Jo and Beth are just about the 'bestest' people she's ever met, and openly wishes her big sister were more like them. I understand and am not offended.

Food is a big deal for them. They talk about it a lot. Jo's a massive meat-eater, but I was bang on about the vegan thing with Beth, and the five years I subsequently spend as a vegan trying to impress her helps with my weight problem. A lot. I think I start to understand why Beth is so thin. And then I get to know her more, and I truly begin to understand why Beth is so thin. Beth used to have a destructive obsessive relationship with food. Occasionally, when we're exceptionally drunk, she speaks about her binge eating issues from her schooldays. Now you may remember I'm a young woman who'll happily sink a loaf of bread in one. So, at first I'm sure I can empathise. Until she describes the volume of food she would secretly pour down and then force out of herself on a regular basis, and I realise I can't. Now she fights those urges by being incredibly careful with food, and she tells me she appreciates life as if she's been reborn, controlling something that used to control her.

I feel included when Beth speaks like this about her troubled past with food, as though she's truly letting me in. But I can tell whenever the subject arises Jo feels terribly uncomfortable. Jo's love for Beth is fierce, and I imagine it's difficult for her to hear about any pain Beth has ever experienced, especially when she hadn't been able to be there for her through it. I also suspect Jo is slightly territorial about this issue, as though only she should be let into this private space of Beth's. I don't want to topple our happy trio dynamic with ugly jealousy, so I usually try to steer away from the topic, and keep my responses to a minimum whenever it surfaces.

But of course I was wrong again. A common occurrence for me when it comes to understanding people.

Our story now picks up where it left off. With Adam offing himself. After Adam's death and subsequent exposure as not quite the guy I'd thought he was, or else so much more than just the guy I'd thought he was, I start going out a lot more. In a kind of pathological way. There's always something to join in with, someone is forever having a house party or heading to a student night, so it's easy to keep busy and keep drunk. I'm miserable, but everyone else simply thinks I've finally become more fun. I've stopped seeing Jo and Beth as frequently because by now they both have jobs they're starting to actually care about, and so can't, or don't want to, accompany me on my student binges. But one day I receive a text from Jo asking if she can join me on my next night out. I'm over the moon as I've missed them, but when Jo turns up alone I realise her text wasn't mis-worded: she meant only she would be joining me. Which is totally fine, of course, except I can't remember the last time I saw Jo without Beth, or vice versa. I don't mention it to Jo for fear of making things awkward. I just enjoy small talk with her and hit the bottle as I've been used to doing for the past few months. But then I notice Jo is doing the same. Exactly the same. Drinking in a desperate and determined way, not the fun way of most drinking companions. Pretty soon I'm drunk enough to ask her what's going on, and although she bats me away at first with jokes and excuses, eventually she gets drunk enough to tell me.

'You really want to know what's wrong?' Jo asks cagily, her face suddenly serious.

I nod.

She looks down at the table and says to it, rather than to me, 'Beth is what's wrong...why she's not here tonight is what's wrong.'

I don't understand, but I stay quiet and frozen in place. I'm not accustomed to Jo being open or solemn, so I worry any sudden movements will make her clam up. Eventually, still looking down, she starts again, slowly at first. 'Beth's not here because she's not allowed to be here...she's not allowed to be anywhere now...except the hospital ...the hospital is the only place she can be safe.' When she looks up at me, I see the tears I could hear in her voice, then it comes out quickly and all at once. 'She's been there for a few weeks now. It's where she sodding lives. She was taken against her will. Because of me. I didn't want to do it, of course I didn't, Jess, but I had to put her there because she kept not eating food, even though I was begging her to just please eat something, and her parents were begging her too. And she kept waking up early every morning and going for long runs, like really, really, long fucking runs, even though her parents and I were begging her to please, please, please, just fucking not. She had got so thin, Jess, so, *so*, thin. The doctors were saying she could drop dead any fucking moment, just die, just like that.' Jo clicks her fingers and stares at me, her eyes desperate.

I still don't think I understand. Beth had always been really thin, but surely she can't have suddenly got *that* thin? What does that thin even look like? Jo shows me a grainy photo of the two of them she took on her phone when she visited Beth at the hospital last night. I find it difficult to look at. It's only their faces, but I can see bits of bone and muscle through Beth's skin that I know I shouldn't be able to see on a live human. She looks ill, literally at death's door, or past the door and sitting on death's sofa, like a smiling corpse. And this is after four weeks of around-the-clock care.

It turns out Jo's awkwardness around the subject of Beth's troubled past with food had nothing to do with jealousy. It was because Jo knew full well Beth's troubled past was in fact a troubled present, a present Jo had been dealing with to greater and lesser extents throughout their now five-year relationship. Anorexia is a secretive disease, it fed on Beth's stories of conquering her past demons, and Jo had been forced to collude in its secrets, biting her tongue whenever the subject of eating arose. She had watched as the disease consumed Beth, and as Beth consumed less and less. But if Jo ever shared her worries with Beth she would be rebuffed, sometimes with a furious anger I couldn't imagine could come from Beth, but from the sadness, exhaustion, and defeat in Jo's eyes, I knew it had. As Jo reveals all of this, she tells me there's relief in finally being able to talk to others about the problem, that this crisis-point at least means she no longer has to bear it all alone.

I learn the control Beth had over her food was disturbing to Jo from the start, but then it became normal to her. So normal she couldn't quite say exactly when the control had started to slowly extend to Jo and all parts of their lives together. Jo's food and time of eating would be policed as strictly as Beth's, but less predictably. Jo had to cook exactly as instructed so as not to ignite Beth's rage. If Jo loved Beth then Jo had to eat more than Beth and more unhealthy foods so as not to make Beth feel like a disgusting fat gluttonous pig. But if Jo loved Beth then Jo also wouldn't eat too much and certainly not too much unhealthy food in front of her so as not to make Beth feel jealous and strange. And Jo had to talk about food with Beth whenever Beth wished, which was eerily frequently. I remember an incident in their flat where we'd discussed taking a trip to Bristol together, a trip which never happened, and Beth found a vegan eatery in the area we could visit on our hypothetical jaunt. I was excited by the idea of a restaurant where I could order absolutely anything on the menu – a rare treat for a vegan, especially back then. But I clearly wasn't as excited as Beth. She read the entire menu aloud to Jo and me, word for word. If she especially liked the sound of a dish, she repeated it. I remember how surreal it felt, but how I'd simply passed it off as maybe something other people like to do; have menu recitals. I remind

Jo of the Bristol story, Beth's insistence on reeling off a whole menu. She doesn't remember it, but she says it sounds about right, a sour laugh catching in her throat.

'For the couple of months before I put her in there, we were visiting the doc twice a week together for weigh-ins and blood tests.' she says. The thought of the skeletal version of Beth I saw in the picture regularly giving away precious blood makes my head swim. She can't spare any life force. 'I was happy to have the doctors involved, y'know, because I thought finally now they were going to fix it. Like, once the experts were on it, she was surely meant to be getting better,' Jo continues, 'But she wasn't, it wasn't working, she was only getting worse. Every time we went, she promised she would do better, try harder, eat more, but she just kept on losing and losing and losing the weight. She was disappearing, Jess, just fucking disappearing.' At this, Jo begins to properly sob. It's only natural of course, the sobbing, but I'm still shocked to see her this way. I'm used to Jo the joker, Jo the strident campaigner, Jo the problem solver. Not Jo the vulnerable, Jo the helpless. I've never even witnessed her shed a single tear before, let alone break down like this. Truthfully, I'd long considered her to be a fellow egg, hardened to the world by an upbringing I gather wasn't all sunshine and lollipops, so it's truly painful to see her so exposed, and it's difficult to know how to respond. I cautiously inch my chair closer to hers and rest my arm around her shoulder, half expecting her to shrug it off, but instead she leans into me. We stay this way for some time, as she pours out her fears with her head against my chest. She's so scared. Scared Beth will never recover. Scared Beth will die. Scared it will be her fault because she couldn't fix her, because she wasn't enough to make Beth better, to make her value their lives together enough to eat. Scared Beth will never forgive Jo for letting her be caged like an animal.

'It's horrific, that place.' Jo says, describing what she sees on her regular visits, 'The patients rant and rave and throw their food around like crazy people. She doesn't belong there, she shouldn't be locked up with those nutters.' I think but don't say that Beth is every bit as sick as them. If she'd rather be hospitalized and put Jo through this than eat a sandwich, Beth needs the same help those people do. It worries me Jo doesn't see this, but I try to be there for her as best I can, this night, and in the days and nights to come.

Beth doesn't die in hospital. Not this first time, anyway. She slowly puts on weight until she's allowed home for weekends, and then eventually full-time. I naively think the treatment has worked, that it's the beginning of a better life for them both. And for a few weeks it seems like it is. But then the cycle begins again. I start to see less and less of them, until again I hear from Jo that Beth has been hospitalised.

This is how it goes.

This is the pattern.

Beth's fourth hospitalization happens over the time of my final university exams. I take time out of my revision to visit her with Jo. The weather is beautiful and my eyes are itchy from pollen as we sit on the grass in the hospital's garden. Beth has put on a little weight, which means I don't find it so difficult to look at her face, although I still can't linger on her arms or legs for very long. She's asking me about girls and books and my exams and the Masters I'll study next year, and with the, and with the sun shining like this, and with her sunglasses covering the hollows under her eyes, we could almost be three normal friends catching up in a regular way in a regular garden for regular people. It's nice. Or as nice as it can be. Then Jo has to take a call from work. She says she'll be two secs, but Beth and I both know she'll be gone a while.

This is when the mood changes. The sun is still out, but with Jo gone the vibe experiences a total eclipse. Beth lies back flat on the grass, which is long overdue a mow. She's so thin she looks like a body half sunk into the earth, and the illusion is so real I have to stop myself from pouncing on her and pulling her back up.

She turns her head and whispers so softly as to be barely audible. 'Promise you'll help Jo find someone else when I'm gone.'

I'm sure I've misheard. I try to make myself mishear. But she repeats her plea.

'Jo hasn't laid eyes let alone hands on anyone else since you got together,' is my light-hearted attempt to reassure her, 'and you being in here isn't going to change that. Jo's the most loyal person I know, but if she were ever tempted to do something stupid in front of me, I'd punch her and the something stupid she was tempted to do.'

Beth smiles weakly. She does everything weakly now. She tells me she's not defeated yet, but she knows she will be. She tells me Jo is her everything, which is precisely why she can't take over her life, ruin her life, the way she has been doing, forever. She tells me Jo will be devastated at first, but eventually she'll be happier than she ever could be with her. She tells me Jo will have a normal life, normal pleasures. She tells me she wants me to make sure of that, that I have to get Jo through the hard bits so she can enjoy the good.

I try to tell her to stop being silly. To buck up. I try to tell her she's a survivor. That she's going to fight this disease and we're going to be there for her every step of the way. That Jo is happy with Beth. That she would never be happier with anyone else. But I can't. As tears fill my eyes and a lump fills my throat, all I can do is nod my agreement.

A year and two more hospitalisations later, Beth holds me to my promise. The day after being re-admitted to the ward her heart finally gives out. The doctors suspect she was doing jumping jacks in her room. Fucking jumping jacks. Jo's heart gives out too, but she has to keep walking around with it.

Beth had left strict instructions with Jo for the funeral. She knew this day was coming and she wanted it to be right. So Jo has to be firm with Beth's parents on the arrangements. And it's worth it. As I sit in the front row of the church holding Jo's hand, I think the whole thing has been choreographed like the wedding Beth will never have. It's so beautiful, so calming, so poignant, so Beth. It's a shame she isn't here to see her plan come to fruition. But she is here of course. And I don't mean that watching over us bullshit. I mean literally here. Her body. Or what's left of it. In there. At the front. In the coffin. The pretty coffin. I didn't know they could be this pretty. It's made out of a kind of straw or wicker material.

Light and beautiful and feminine. With the yellow bow and flowers on top, it looks like an Easter basket.

I'm glad I declined the request to give a reading as my tears flow unrelentingly throughout the service. I'm standing still, but I'm falling into a hole. I can feel it. First Adam, and now this. I'm scared of losing myself to these tears. Scared they'll never stop. I can't catch my breath. I don't want to hyperventilate and ruin the ceremony for everyone. I try to find something to focus my attention, something to keep me together. I try reciting the hymn numbers on the wall over and over in my mind. I try digging my fingernails into my palms and concentrating on the pain. I try tracing the patterns of the stained-glass windows with my eyes. But nothing works. Until I notice something small on the pew's ledge in front of me. It's difficult to make out at first, but when we're next asked to sit down I can see it's the desiccated body of a bee. A thin little worker bee. It's been there so long it's broken into three parts, each shrivelled and dry. I inspect it thoroughly. I become engrossed, and my tears subside somewhat. I silently name all the body parts I can see. The head containing the mandibles and the compound eye. The thorax with the detached paper-thin wings, hind and fore. The legs, hind, middle, fore. The abdomen, the spiracles, the sting. The sting.

The sting.

The sting.

I wonder how it got there, to its final resting place in this house of worship. It has a story. Maybe its story is one of bravery, of selflessness and sacrifice, of giving up its life to save its hive and queen, like the bees I learned about at university. But ultimately, now it's a body. Just a body becoming dust. No different to my friend's body lying a few feet away. We think we're special but we're not. We're animals and then we're dust.

And that's when the click happens, I guess.

I see it clearly.

I will stay strong by keeping my promise to Beth. Together Beth and I will make sure Jo, her queen, has a happier life. Beth by leaving it. Me by staying in it. And the click brings something else. I decide to stay strong by learning more about death and suicide. Suicide in animals is suicide in us. The week after the funeral I turn down the PhD place I have been offered to study the genetics of asthma and apply for one studying altruistic suicide in insects and arachnids.

My pact with Beth works. After years of mourning, Jo goes on to marry a woman she meets at a terrible gay club I drag her along to. I am her maid of honour. They have two children. They are wonderful mothers. Their children have a stable and happy home. Jo misses Beth. We remember her together.

But Jo is happy.

A BLACK DAY

I've got five choices. All new. I'll pick just one. A costume change would be a tad gauche, I think. I'll return the rest.

I try them on, one after the other, in front of my bedroom mirror. I walk wearing each of them in turn to look in the spare room's mirror, her mirror, because the light is different in there. More natural. Less flattering. It's probably important to try to see things as they really are, even if how things really are is I look awful.

The first is too lacy. Inappropriate for me, for today. The second is too tight. I've lost a lot of weight recently, but in a bad way and in the wrong places, and the second outfit manages to make me look too fat and too thin all at once. Quite a feat, really. Almost makes me want to choose it. The third outfit gives the impression I'm off to a job interview for the kind of job I'd never want. The fourth is a dress. Very off-brand. Why did I buy a dress? The fifth is ok. Bit fun though. I don't want people to think I'm having fun.

I'm not sure I can do this. I know I can't do it in any of these outfits. I don't want to be looked at in any of these outfits.

I search through my wardrobe for the thing I think I wore to the last one. It still fits. It looks fine. Adequate.

Maybe I can do it in this.

A FAILURE

The successes of Adam and Beth, successfully killing themselves, that is, were significant influences on my life and my work. But it's my original brush with suicide's failure that plagues me most, that most strongly gives me these feelings I keep to myself, the feeling that suicide is sometimes nature's way of doing the right thing by the ones you love. My father, the failure in every way, is my biggest inspiration.

Now I don't know what kind of story it is I'm writing here, or if strictly speaking I'm even writing a story at all. Perhaps that's already become clear to you? But whatever it is I'm disclosing, or putting down, or off-loading, or committing, or whatever, I can tell you what it isn't. It isn't a poor-little-me abuse porno. This isn't where I describe in minute detail the years of cruelty that made me the warped monster I am today. I won't paint a vivid picture of suffering to make you thankful for your beige upbringing, or if you were one of the unlucky ones, to act as a trigger or to make you feel closer to me through our shared trauma. I'm not going to give you, or him, or anyone, that. I recognise I have to put something on the record though, something to make you understand..

So I will try.

I'll start by saying my dad didn't fuck me. Not even once. So get your mind out of the gutter. And to the best of my knowledge he didn't fuck my brother or sister either. I've never asked them though, and they have always been far more attractive than I, so I guess it's always a possibility. I imagine it's something most people give little thought to, but I for one am very grateful my father didn't fuck me. I try to always remember that lots of people have had it a hell of a lot worse than I did.

I do know he fucked my mum on occasion, obviously, and I believe it was always with her consent. But he wasn't always such a sweet guy. He also broke her jaw. And another time her ribs. I once saw him drag her along the floor by her hair. Another time he ripped her dress in two and strangled her in the kitchen. Her neck had bruises and scratches that took weeks to fully heal. He once threw my brother down the stairs. Only halfway down really, so it sounds worse than it was. Although he still broke his arm. He once punched me in the face. I got two black eyes, but it only bruised rather than broke my nose. Thank goodness, as my already outsized nose didn't need any help drawing the eye. So to be fair to my father, who is a larger than average guy, he clearly didn't punch me as hard as he was able to. He once literally threw me out on to the street. I fractured my ankle where it hit the curb, and I had to limp to a friend's house to spend the night. Pretty embarrassing. He once stabbed me in the thumb with a sardine can lid. They're really bloody sharp, and the cut stank of fish as I waited for hours in A&E to get it stitched up. Kind of a funny story I guess. Although maybe you had to be there.

But these flashes of actual physical person-on-person violence causing actual direct physical bodily harm were relatively rare. I can probably list them all on two hands. Maybe four or five hands. But rare nonetheless. Rare compared to the insults. Rare compared to the rage. Rare compared to the ranting. Rare compared to the threats. Rare compared to the seething hatred. Rare compared to the fear that was more or less a constant feature of my childhood.

My father worked shifts. So he didn't have to keep regular hours. This meant the fear didn't keep regular hours either. You couldn't take a break from it at night. In fact, a whole lot of his ranting happened at night. If you've never experienced it, I can tell you that if you're trying to carve out a run-of-the-mill existence for yourself, maybe prepare for exams, rest up before a date, recover from a night out, it's very inconvenient to have your door ripped off its hinges, again, at three in the morning. It's terribly exhausting to have your bedcovers dragged off you frequently throughout the night. It's quite unsettling to have your father's spit hitting your face as he kneels down next to your bed and screams abuse at you for the umpteenth time that evening. It does nothing for your beauty sleep to be listening to the rage when it's in your mother's room, having to stay constantly alert in case it tips over the edge where you need to call the police. Again.

But my father dearest was no vampire. His rage occurred just as frequently during daylight hours. What nighttime rage is to sleep, daytime rage is to pride. You see, daytime rage is trickier to contain, and therefore more often seen by others. It's hard to hold your head high when people have seen your dad smashing your guitar and calling you a pathetic talentless waste of space because you had the nerve to let your friends wait outside the house while you get changed before heading out again, rather than the far preferable option of never bringing anyone anywhere near the house, and not having any friends in the first place. It's tough to play the cool kid when your dad has caused a scene at the school play, storming out halfway through and dragging your mum behind him. Although I would like to state for the record that given the circumstances, my narration – I was always the narrator, never the star – barely faltered. It's almost impossible to overcome the shame of people you know witnessing your dad losing his cool in a supermarket, smashing jars and making threats, and calling you a stupid whore who will never amount to anything.

So that was my world. A world in which it was difficult to get sleep, and even harder to get self-esteem. But I somehow got both, or enough of them both to function. Living like this was normal to me, but I knew it wasn't everyone's normal. I looked around me and I learned what most people's normal was. I don't just mean the lack of rage and violence. I knew that wasn't normal pretty early on. I mean the subtler stuff. It took longer, but gradually it seeped in. The most epiphany-like moment came when I was twelve and my classmate Hannah suggested we hang out the following weekend. I must've said, 'Sure that sounds like fun.' Then as the weekend approached, she mentioned it again, like it was really going to happen.

'Oh, so you'd actually meant it?' I asked. 'You actually want to hang out? We're actually doing this?'

She was annoyed. Of course she meant it and wanted it to happen, otherwise she wouldn't have said it. And so we hung out that weekend.

I know that's a fairly uneventful story. There won't be a bidding war for the film rights. But it slapped me in the face at the time, and twenty years on it's still stuck with me. I think about all the times our family plans were cancelled because my dad decided to tear the house down with his rage. I think about all the times he fooled us, and we oh-so-very-nearly got to the place we said we were going to be. And then at the last minute he would stop the car and throw my mum out. He'd then drive at her as fast as he could and swerve off just at the last minute. Not even going through with that plan. He really was a very good driver, it must be said. Unless he was actually trying to hit her. Then not so much. It isn't an earth-shattering story, I know, but by hanging out with me on a Saturday when I was twelve, as planned, Hannah taught me that most people go through with their plans, and that I should too.

I must've learned other things from all the more normal people who surrounded me too. Picking up on the way of the *normals* so I could attempt to pass for one of them. Because on balance, all things considered, I ended up being pretty darn good at passing for normal. Much like a photo of a high-quality wax celebrity sculpture, if you don't spend too much time looking at me, I can pass for the real thing. But even then, even when you totally and utterly believe you're looking at a photo on social media of your friend with the actual real John flipping Travolta next to them, even if as you scroll past that picture onto a photo of your workmate's newly adopted rescue cat with the missing eye – bloody Susan showing all of Instagram she's a flipping saint – and you're still totally convinced and none the wiser as to the waxiness of that John

Travolta you just saw, you still find yourself thinking that although you do really still love John Travolta – of course you do, he's so talented, a triple threat – it really is a shame it seems there's something a bit off about him nowadays. So yeah, that's me. I appear almost normal, only a bit off.

Being a bit off used to upset me. Of course I wanted to be normal. Doesn't everyone? But I've come to see being only a *bit* off as pretty good going. In evaluating the success of an outcome, you must account for the starting point. When I was twenty-four I attended a conference seminar on the effects of childhood trauma. It had very little to do with my work, but so did all the other talks in that particular timeslot, and it seemed the least boring, and it felt too early in the day to just bunk off completely and explore New York. I'd anticipated hearing about how people who'd spent their childhoods caged in a basement, or being screwed by their maths teacher, or being child stars, became truly disturbed adults. But instead I heard about the effects of childhoods like mine. Or maybe even childhoods that weren't quite as bad as mine. *Chaotic households,* they called them, or *harsh parenting households.* Places where angry language is used, where there's no routine, where there's mess, where there's fear and anxiety. Check, check, check, and check.

I'm not crazy, I knew the old violent childhood stuff wasn't exactly great. I'd removed myself from that sort of environment as soon as I could, running away to university, and then to slum-like shared accommodation with strangers afterwards. And sure, I got away from the acute harm, from the sleep deprivation, from the physical violence. But the conference taught me there's no real escape. I won't ever be free of those early influences because they have chronic effects. I learned from this lecture, and from the hours of frantic research I did following it, that people who grow up surrounded by chaos and fear are more likely to live adult lives full of chaos and fear. More likely to suffer anxiety, depression, addiction. Maybe that's predictable. Maybe I knew that really. But there was more than that, because an unhealthy early environment leads to unhealthy adult bodies – with people like me more likely to suffer cancer, heart disease, and auto-immune disorders. Maybe you think of course they're more likely to be unhealthy if they're more depressed and they're drinking more? Well no. Because these scientists have shown that when you stress out young mice, they go on to have screwed up minds and bodies, and that certainly isn't because they spend too much time in the pub. The stress re-wires them, messing up their hormones and their immune system. In that lecture, knowledge I'd always held in my body, somewhere in my gut, transferred to my brain: people who grew up like I did, our wiring is and will always be wrong.

This knowledge helped me in my work. I started to accept the thoughts I'd been having about suicide and its utility. I started to see myself as living proof that suicide could be a good thing, and that failing to top yourself, as my father had, could have detrimental effects on your kin. When I was sat in that conference at twenty-four years old, I'd recently been diagnosed with urticaria. It basically means itchy skin. I have itchy skin. All over. All the time. I take antihistamines every day, and that makes it a lot better. I've been taking them every day now for over ten years. If I don't take them I eventually break out in hives. When I was twenty-nine, after complaining for years of dry eyes, a dry mouth, and – sorry for the TMI moment here – a dry vagina, I was eventually diagnosed with Sjörgen syndrome. My immune system is so utterly juiced and stressed and ready for action that it's started attacking my own body. For now it's attacking those bits which produce fluid, my tear glands and salivary glands, and who knows what it'll go for next. This usually affects people in their forties, fifties and sixties. I developed it in my twenties. There's no way the doctors can conclusively tell why I developed it so early. But I know why. It's because by the time I left home at eighteen my body had already been through more than any decent lifetime's worth of stress, anxiety, and fear.

Relatively speaking though, as long as I don't develop non-Hodgkin's lymphoma, the likelihood of which is increased by my Sjörgen syndrome, or full-blown lupus, I got off pretty lightly. I own my own flat. It's not perfect, sure. It's quite dusty because I find dusting mind-numbingly boring. My frizzy thick hair malts a lot and I don't hoover quite often enough to prevent the occasional weird build-up of hairballs on my carpet. And it's difficult to ever get my shower properly spotless because it's hard to get behind the shower door, you know? But other than that it's fairly clean and tidy and normal looking. I set my alarm every evening and I wake up after a few snoozes every morning and I show up only about ten to fifteen minutes late every day for my job. I frequently stay at work very late though, so I think it evens out, and my boss seems to agree. I meet most of my deadlines, and manage to shift those I don't. I have friends who have good jobs and beautiful homes and loving families. I see them regularly and laugh and joke with them. Sometimes I even invite them into my flat. Not often, because it makes me very stressed to have people in my space. But I've had them here a few times and I've cooked for them and I think it's always gone well. It's never been my dream to travel, and yet I've visited numerous countries in the world, many of which were the locations of work conferences and so my travel was free. I can't drive. But I live in London, so who needs a car?

So, in the shitty-childhood sample of three that is me and my siblings, one third of us is living an ok if rather dry and itchy life. If it were just me, maybe I wouldn't have seen my family reflected in that lecture, or maybe I wouldn't have cared so much. But it isn't just me. And the other two thirds aren't exactly smashing it. Life, that is. Even back when I was twenty-four some of the effects mentioned in the lecture were starting to become apparent. Over ten years on and between them they're doing a cracking job working their way through the entire list of emotional and behavioural problems that come with having a warped starting point.

When I was in that talk all those years ago I felt like the speaker was directly addressing me. Like they were giving me a rundown of my history and painting a picture of my future. *That* talk at *that* conference changed things for me. I started working harder, and perhaps only half-consciously at first, looking for evidence with fresh eyes, evidence to back up my theory. As my physical, and my siblings' mental, health declined, my conviction only became stronger. I started following those suicidal spiders, the *Atypena lentil*, more closely, despite how much their spindly little legs creeped me out, looking for something that maybe only someone like me could look for. And when I found what I was looking for, as all evolutionary psychologists and biologists eventually do, I felt this was my calling. As awful as it was, I even started to feel some small amount of pride in my past, because it had given me the capacity to see the evolutionary benefit of something as dark as suicide. A discovery like that wasn't for someone normal to unearth, someone good, it was for someone like me. My childhood had sharpened my mind and deadened my emotions enough to make me less attached to human life than I might otherwise have been. I guess even back then I knew I was the metaphorical egg, not the coffee bean or even the carrot. And I was glad, at that time, to be an egg. Only an egg could do the work I was doing.

A WEDNESDAY

An alarm is sounding for the fifth time, which means I've had my snooze allowance for the morning. Four times already my heart has sunk as the fog of sleep cleared enough for me to remember it's a Wednesday. Now my heart sinks for the fifth time. Wednesday is the worst day. Not only will I be seeing him today, but also the next day, the next day, and the one after that. At least Sunday, Monday, and Tuesday are mine alone. I rise, wipe sleep from my eyes, and start moving through the worst day.

After work I catch the bus to the sheltered accommodation. I toy with the idea, as always, of missing my stop, and remaining on the bus to see what the world is like past this depressing edge. As always, I decide against it just in time to hop through the doors as they close. I walk to the entrance of the beige, structured community, where Arthur the security guard sits behind his plastic window. There's a rope cordon, which, although I'm never here on Sundays, I understand sometimes comes in handy on the day of rest if a small queue develops when more visitors arrive than Arthur can process at one time. Apparently it is also the day of familial, or perhaps guilty, feelings. As usual, there's no queue on this particular Wednesday evening, so I approach the window directly. And as usual, Arthur directs me to walk through the cordoned queue area.

'But there's no queue today, Arthur.'

'Rules are rules, please queue this way,' he replies.

Does Arthur realise this has become our routine? Is he joking? Am I? Jamie used to find me relaying this interaction hilarious, me doing the actions and putting on Arthur's gruff serious tone, but it's not quite as funny now on my own. As always, I feign embarrassment at my mistake and do as he says, and he lets me enter the *secure* premises, which I could have entered fairly easily via several different points without his permission. I appreciate the tiny spots of manicured garden outside some of the units, struggling somewhat in the heat of this summer's evening, until I reach the un-manicured number 13.

Unlucky for some.

I let myself in and find my dad sleeping in front of some variety of sport. I heard it blaring from outside the front door before I even entered. I turn down the volume, open all the windows to unfairly exchange some fresh air for this hot mess of an atmosphere, and head to the kitchen, which is a rather grand term for one small worksurface and a microwave.

He won't be happy, but a salad is all I feel up to making and eating on an evening like this. I open the bag of watercress, remove a tangle, and tear shreds of green into a bowl. I've read watercress is incredibly good for you. It's apparently anti-carcinogenic and good for the thyroid gland, the heart, and bones. It even has antidepressant effects. But deep down I know I bought it for none of these reasons. I bought it because he hates it. I peel and grate two carrots with some difficulty, as they've become a little soft, and add shiny plum tomatoes from the vine. As I open and drain a can of artichokes, and add some prepared chicken, sun-dried tomatoes, capers, olive oil and vinegar, I look over at him with his head lolled back in sleep and think of slicing his neck open with the Japanese weighted blade I paid a fortune for that I hold in my hand. I have these thoughts when I look at him from time to time. If looks could kill, he'd be coughing up blood right now. But I'm simply looking, and he's simply snoring.

It's not always like this. Sometimes I look at him and I experience such overwhelming pity I have to turn away to hide the tears filling my eyes. These warmer sentimental moods make me far more uncomfortable than the murderous ones, and they're harder to explain, even to myself. But they must be natural I guess, because I suspect Freya shares them. She would never say it, but I think I've seen it in her face. When the doctors first called to tell me about his deterioration, and I then quickly discovered what a hovel his house had become, Freya agreed to help me clean it for him. She made it very plain she was doing this for me though, *not* for him, because she told me the only thing that made her angrier than helping me clean up his shit was the thought of me having to clean up his shit all alone. She reminded me of how incensed she was the *entire* time we were cleaning, which took over two weeks in all. She was livid she had to be elbow deep in his grime, livid she was doing for him what she felt he would never have done for her, livid that even now he was ruining her life when she could be off having fun. Each scrub of her sponge was a blow to his head, each thrust of the hoover a sword through his heart. It became sort of amusing really, her rage. Amusing and useful. It made her a great cleaner. When I was exhausted on the sofa at the end of each day, she was still using her vitriol to polish the place to an aggressive shine.

Freya agreed to help only on the condition that she didn't have to see him. Which seemed possible as he'd been kept in hospital for observations, then biopsies, then recovery, and then for his own safety. But the drugs they gave him started to have a particularly positive effect and he was let out slightly earlier than we expected, which meant their paths did in fact cross briefly one evening. And that's when I saw it. Freya's shock at what he had become. Followed by the pity, the sadness, the grief. I didn't ask her what the look meant, because I knew. It meant she would rather he'd remained the monster in her mind, than become…this. It meant she shared the same confusion I did. Confusion because, well, I didn't think I'd care so much. Or care at all. Perhaps I'm wrong, it remains to be seen, but I truly don't think I will be all that upset when he dies. In the years before he fell ill I hardly saw him, and it often felt like the ideal state would be never having to see him again. So, I don't think it's the death bit that's the issue for me, or for Freya. It's his life, his life as it is now, that hurts. It's like seeing a once terrifying dog – a dog that was formerly all muscle and teeth and rage, a dog that used to mercilessly maul rabbits for fun – on its last legs. I can't help but grieve the lost power, and pity what now stands in its place.

I think Freya felt the same way too that day. It may be partly why she hasn't seen him since, and why she helped me select this sheltered community and interview the carer who visits him on the days I don't without *too many* complaints. Although of course, as expected, her promised financial contribution to said carer never materialised. My dad is a shadow of his former self. He has shrunk. And his newfound docility, his confusion, his compliance, his helplessness, it's sometimes all too much to bear.

Is it because of *love* that it hurts so much to see him this way?

I don't think so. Or at least *love* is too broad a term for this particular thing.

How can the same word be used to describe what I feel, what I felt, for Jamie, and what I feel for my dad? No, it's not love, not that same love anyway. It's a far less conditional, far more animal tie. It's the primal pull of family, of shared genetics. It's the fact his features are my features, his blood is my blood. It makes me feel things that my brain, with all its knowledge of my dad and the things he's done, can't comprehend. But it's ok. Whenever this maudlin mood strikes I simply look up, breathe deeply, bite my bottom lip, and console myself in the certainty that I'll soon swing back to resentment.

And sure enough, I always do.

When I'm done in the kitchen I place the bowl next to him on his tray, nudge his shoulder and take my place in the other armchair. He wakes, nods acknowledgement to me and eats the salad in silence while we watch the sport highlights. I detest sport, so does everyone in my family apart from my dad. I think this is precisely why everyone else hates it, because he loves it, but it's a difficult theory to prove. No point hypothesising what you cannot test. I blankly stare at the screen, refusing to take anything in. I impress myself with my will. So often in my life I have sat in a house with sport commentary blaring from a TV or a radio nearby, and yet I proudly cannot answer one single sports question in even the easiest of pub quizzes. Quite an achievement, I'd say. So, we sit together as he eats a dinner he hates and I watch TV I hate. When we're done eating I clear our plates and read while my dad continues to watch TV and snooze. I forgot to bring my book today, so instead I pick up one of the magazines the carer tends to leave lying around. I rarely read women's magazines anymore, and I'm surprised anew by the number of ways it is possible for a woman's body to be wrong. Of course, the tone has changed somewhat since my youth. We're into self-love and body positivity, now, right? But it seems we're also into shaving our faces for extra smoothness, contouring until we're unrecognisable, and tackling underboob sweat head-on. And of course, we still like gawping at those women who've had the audacity to undergo too much self-improving weight loss or plastic surgery.

I'm reminded that it's absorbing, the self-hatred thing, the picking-apart-women's-bodies-to-evaluate-them thing. As an evolutionary researcher I know it's a natural part of being human, evaluating oneself, evaluating potential mates, evaluating the competition. The literature even suggests a worthy note to the endeavour, as some have shown the same part of our brain that judges moral ugliness, judges physical ugliness too. No wonder I become so engrossed in the magazine's ethical revulsion to celebrity crow's feet and tips on how to apply eyeliner to achieve the noblest effect. Before I know it ninety minutes have passed and it's nearly time for me to leave. Except, damn it, I remember the regular carer is away for the week so Dad likely hasn't had a bath since the weekend. Fantastic.

'Dad,' I shout, jolting him from a snooze, 'time for a bath.'

He groggily reaches for his frame on wheels and slowly pulls himself up. My dad can barely walk now, his knees and ankles apparently having been worn away from years of fanatical exercise and angrily terrorising a house full of his nearest and dearest. To be fair to the man, have you ever tried angrily raging while standing completely still in one spot? It's incredibly difficult to do, although it might be worth a try if you rage regularly and value your knees. He had a hip replacement three years ago that was supposed to at least help with some of the pain, but it didn't quite go to plan, and after infections, detachments, and bone erosion, on balance the hip is worse today than it was in his pre-operation days. He can still, mercifully, usually bathe himself, especially as the flats in this complex all come equipped with handrails and walk-in tubs as standard. Except currently his ankle is in a cast after a nasty fall. He can't get the cast wet and showering or bathing without getting a cast wet requires a nimbleness he lost long ago. So, I think, as I help him into the bathroom, it'll probably have to be a sponge bath. I haven't had to bathe him since just after the first hip operation and back then he was so out-of-it it wasn't terribly awkward. Or maybe that's just how I feel in retrospect – I think bathing your own aged father must always be a tad awkward – but this is the moment I'm in, and so this is the most awkward moment, of course.

After a lot of ungraceful shuffling about, I hit upon a plan. I help him out of his clothes, open the walk-in-bath's door, and ease him into a position where most of him is in the bath apart from his cast leg which is trailing on the bathroom floor side. I then wet and soap a sponge in the bathroom sink and hand it to him to wash the areas within his reach. This includes, thank all that is good, the most problematic area, which as I stand focusing my attention elsewhere, I am sure I can hear flopping around while it is cleansed. Everything has shrunk with age, apart from his earlobes, so imagine the sound of a very small fish, maybe a goldfish or an anchovy, slapping against a rock.

I wonder why I feel such shame in this moment. Sure, when I imagine stabbing him with an expensive Japanese knife, I know it's something I would never do, but why can't I use this moment to take out some measure of revenge? Why don't I shame this little old man who has been the largest evil in my life? I could surely do that? Pay him back for the shame he brought on me. Have you read Caitlin Moran's *How to be a Woman?* She discusses the notion that most females first realise they're crossing or have crossed the bridge between girl and womanhood because some random man shouts sexist abuse at them in the street. *Nice tits love*, and the like. That idea of the threshold to womanhood being a slap in the face really rang true to me, except I wasn't in the street, I was at home. And that man wasn't a stranger, he was my dad.

I was a rather early developer. I started my period when I was ten, and my breasts and pubic hair started appearing a couple of years before that. I later learned this was no chance occurrence, as studies have shown early-life stress is associated with early menarche. And lucky me, early menarche is associated with early menopause, increased rates of breast and ovarian cancers, depression, substance abuse, sexual risk taking and teenage pregnancy – although I guess that last one never posed too much of a risk for me personally. So imagine me at eight. I've come home from school and have run up to my room to change into my home clothes before heading back down to watch *Saved by the Bell*, my favourite show. I open my drawer and am happy to find my favourite pyjamas have been washed. They're a blue and purple patchwork matching t-shirt and shorts with a grey bear on the left breast's pocket. I'm overjoyed I can wear my favourite PJs, so I pop them on, even though last time I wore them the top button had been lost. My mum said she'd have to sew on another one, but I'm not too bothered by that, it's a pretty warm day. I've got my PJs on and I'm running down the stairs and as I near the bottom my dad appears and starts to ascend. He does that thing he does where he doesn't let me pass, but today I can tell he's in a dark mood and is doing it in the aggressive way not the funny way.

'What the fuck are you wearing?' he says.

I'm relieved because this is an easy question to which I know the answer, and I'm pretty happy about said answer too, so I tell him that I'm wearing my favourite cuddly bear pyjamas.

'Are you trying to turn me on you little slut?' is his reply.

Now, in many ways I am a relatively clued up child by this point. To my benefit, and my detriment, my parents' unpredictable and disordered household is one where I can stay up late and watch adult shows whenever I want. Therefore I have a healthy fear of strangers based far more on the real-life crimes I have seen reconstructed on Crimewatch than on the rather catchy tune about saying no to strangers our teacher plays us at school. I also have a remarkably mature vocabulary, which teachers refuse to believe I acquired through the wonders of television and not through reading. So, I know what being turned on is, and I know what a slut is, but I really can't understand why these things are being said to me, a kid in pyjamas, by my dad. But as I enquire, he just keeps repeating the same questions, getting angrier each time. Eventually my mum finds us like this, and…you've guessed it, she tells me off for wearing my t-shirt before she has fixed it, and sends me upstairs to get changed.

That was when I realised I'd grown breasts. Breasts which had appeared so rapidly I hadn't noticed. And I guess that was my first taste of being a woman: receiving sexist abuse, and then being told I was asking for it because of my sartorial choices.

Thanks Dad.

But even as the old arsehole washes his old arsehole with a sponge in front of me, I still can't muster up the…the what? Courage? Animosity? Venom? Energy? The whatever-it-takes to shame him back. I simply continue to hand the old broken dog the re-dampened sponge over my shoulder until he's done. I help him get dressed and I leave without saying goodbye, feeling grateful that at least we won't have to do that again for a while.

A BLACK DAY

He looks smart as they wheel him in, all in black. I chose those clothes. I bought them especially. None of his suits fit anymore. They belonged to the bigger him. I went for black everything: a black suit, a black shirt, a black tie, a black pocket square, black socks, black shoes. Black is how this feels. All light absorbed. For some reason I wanted to be the one to dress him and although it was frankly rather inconvenient, I rushed over beforehand to be involved.

I thought I'd still be angry. Angrier than ever. But I wasn't. I'm not. I seem to have let it all go, even if I hadn't wanted to.

A HOPE

'Why do you do it to yourself?' Jamie always asks. Meaning, why do I continue to visit this person I apparently have nothing but ill will towards, instead of coming home early and enjoying only good will with her?

I don't know the answer.

Jamie asks a lot of questions. She wants to get to the bottom of everything. In a different way to me. She wants emotions. She wants change. She wants personal analysis, and more importantly, she wants personal development. She wants evolution, not evolutionary psychology. And she wants to make plans. She wants to look ahead, not backwards. I guess opposites attract.

Our first meeting is at a terrible gay night full of sweaty bears with their tops off. As two of the very few women in the club we are all but forced to at least briefly notice one another. Which works massively in my favour, as she is the most beautiful woman I have ever seen and I have no doubt she wouldn't even deign to look at me if there were any other options around. Our gazes graze and my heart skips. She is wearing all black. But not in the way I frequently wear all black for ease of washing, coordination, and blending into the background. She's wearing all black with purpose, with flair, to court rather than escape attention. Her outfit is sleek and deliberate, simple and androgynous. It's a statement. It's an identity. Each time I clock her dancing with her friends I feel my pulse quicken and make a mental note of the hottie. I then of course leave that mental note right where it is – in my mind – without ever dreaming of speaking to her or even mentioning her to my pals, for fear they may force me into awkward stranger danger. However, in room five of the five-room bear pit, she inexplicably starts dancing towards our group. She's on her own now and although she's playing it pretty cool, she is gradually but definitely getting closer. I assume she's heading over for Laura, as everyone heads over for Laura because Laura is a tall, blonde, boyish femme with effortless I-just-washed-and-went hair, who doesn't wear a bra and doesn't care if you know it. Laura's a bit of an obvious choice for such a mysterious and glamourous woman in black, and a totally understandable one at that. But if she *is* into Laura, why is this girl repeatedly making eye contact with *me*, forcing me to look away with embarrassment each time? Is she doing that thing where you include all the ugly friends in the group so your real target doesn't feel too targeted? I've never tried it, having never knowingly pursued a *target* before, but I've heard about it and can imagine it to be an effective technique. I decide that must be her game but then when I glance back over, I think if that's really her strategy shouldn't she be looking at Laura at least a little bit? And also at the other uglies in our group too, who are of course not actually ugly in the slightest but, like me, are also no Lauras. It's becoming clear this woman in black is looking directly at *me* and at very little else. As she gets nearer her stare is so intense I feel my face becoming warm and I have to subtly dab at my top lip to keep it dry. Everyone else in the group has now started to notice and they are giving me totally unashamedly conspicuous nudges and winks, further exacerbating the perspiration situation. She sidles over so there is only one person between us and continues her fixed gaze, and when that person decides to go to the bar, leaving nothing but sweaty smoke-filled air between us, I find it all so excruciatingly awkward I am compelled to speak first.

My voice squeaks as I nervously vomit out a 'Hi', but I soon learn there's no need to be nervous. She's a pro. She puts me at ease as soon as she opens her mouth, her affability immediately rendering her beauty less intimidating. She introduces herself, poses lots of questions, and as we move to lean against a wall in a quieter area she seems genuinely interested in the answers, in me, in my work, in the crappy area where I live, in my friends and in my plans for the future, of which I of course have very few. I find I enjoy talking about these familiar things with her, seeing myself reflected anew in her eyes, but I'm hungry for information too. I find out her name. It's Jamie. I think the way it's gender-neutral, and the fact it also sounds vaguely French, suits her. I like the way the name feels in my mouth. She works sourcing and supplying props for films, but her real passion is art. She's a painter. I can't imagine anything more exciting, but in the way creative types sometimes do she seems to find my scientific work far more glamorous. Of course I love that. We stand there talking for ages, completely ignoring our respective friends as they walk back and forth trying to catch our eyes. I'm so engrossed in our conversation, so keen to hear more about her, that it surprises me when she leans forward and asks if she can kiss me. I can't believe that she, this glorious creature, is asking permission for anything, let alone me. Of course I wholeheartedly give it.

The world disappears. Her mouth on my mouth is everything. Her hand in my hair is everything. Her body against mine is everything. But when she pulls away and asks if I will go back to hers I have a familiar moment of panic. I haven't prepared for this. My legs and armpits are hairy, my bush untrimmed, and I'm pretty sure I'm wearing underwear with cartoons on them, and socks with holes that expose my big toes. Why do I never prepare for this eventuality, for *getting lucky*? I guess it's because when I do, I fear my presumptuousness will jinx things. Damned if I do, damned if I don't. More important than my untended bush or nerd pants, I haven't had sex in ten months. What if I've forgotten how to *do sex*? What if I make the woman in black laugh, not in a good way? On the other hand, what if I don't get this opportunity again for another ten months, and then I really *will* forget? As if she can hear the argument raging inside my head, Jamie assures me she hadn't been expecting this either, and we can just go to hers for a drink and see how it goes.

I follow her back to her place in Haggerston, looking forward to a no pressure drink and trying not to objectify her completely as she climbs the stairs to her apartment in front of me. Her place is unsurprisingly as gorgeous as she is. Clean and tidy but full of unusual items she tells me she picked up to use as props but loved so much she kept them for her flat. She asks if I've seen a particular arthouse film she worked on that featured her drinks globe. The film's far too cool for me to have even heard of, let alone seen. I resist the temptation to lie to impress her and instead simply tell her I've always wanted a drinks globe. Her book collection is astounding. It covers two of the living room walls from floor to ceiling, running across the top of two doorways, and is organised entirely by colour.

I peruse the bookshelves while Jamie fetches our drinks. In the orange hued section I find that bible of our people, *Oranges are not the only fruit,* and I pull it out and finger through it. It's been a long time since I've read it. Over ten years. I'm engrossed in the words when I feel Jamie's hands slip around my waist and her warm breath in my ear as she reads the lines over my shoulder.

'We were quiet, and I traced the outline of her marvellous bones and the triangle of muscle in her stomach. What is it about intimacy that makes it so very disturbing?' Her hands move slowly down my body as she reads and as they do they brush all the anxieties about my unpreparedness away.

I steady myself with my hands on her shelf as she stands behind me, kissing my ears, licking my neck. I am not disturbed by this intimacy. I don't have the presence of mind to be disturbed. In fact, I barely manage to keep it together enough to place her book back on the shelf. Because in her hands I am swimming. Or she is swimming in me because I am melting. Her tongue is on me and I am liquid. Her teeth graze me and I am burning. I am fire. I am floating. I am air. I am disappearing. I am nothing. I am no more thinking, only feeling. And just as my legs are about to give way beneath me and I pour into a puddle on the floor, she spins me around and pins my arms against the bookshelf above my head. She holds me in place, firmly, and moves her mouth softly, teasingly, down my neck, along my collarbone, across my breasts, down, down, down, and then up again to my lips, but skimming them only lightly, so lightly. I reach out for her with my mouth, but she pulls back playfully. I feel unclothed even before she undresses me. And when she does I can feel my wetness against my thighs, and then against her trousers as she slides one leg in between mine. She enters me with her fingers, one, then two, then stretching me open with the third, encircling me with her thumb, blinding me with pleasure as I come against all of those books I'd admired. Then finally she lets me fall to the floor and she falls with me.

I shouldn't have worried about forgetting. My body acts without my brain, my muscles holding all the knowledge I need. I tear through the black until it's gone and I can see all of her. I take her into my mouth and taste her saltiness, her sweetness, the sea of her, the earth of her, the meat of her. I want to consume her. I can feel her riding, pulsing against my tongue, harder and faster until her pleasure is inside of me. Then we hold each other, and I don't care that the floor is cold and hard and wooden, I feel I could lie here with her forever.

Of course we can't lie on her floor forever. We can't even lie in her warm, soft, welcoming bed forever, although over the next few months we make a valiant attempt – minus trips to the fridge for refuelling – at doing just that. No. I am always aware that at some point we will have to take our relationship – because if you keep having sex often enough a relationship is what you have – outside the warm and cosy confines of the bed, the bedroom, and even the flat. We have to attempt to incorporate it into our everyday lives and our existing relationships. I try to put this process off for as long as I can. I opt to meet at her flat after she has work drinks with colleagues, rather than joining her as she had asked. I lie and tell her no partners are invited to my friends' social events. I invent important plans when her parents come to visit. Nevertheless, I know it can't remain just the two of us forever, and my heart sinks at the thought of opening us up, of taking us public, because in my limited experience of two serious girlfriends and four semi-serious flings, this is where the problems start. Two people who are insanely in love in the bubble they create in a bedroom can crumble when transported into the context of a real and boring life, where stress and trouble and complexity exist. After being so close to someone that it's almost hard to see them, it's like stepping back and zooming out. You start to see the person at the macro level, to see their interactions with others, to take off the lust-tinted spectacles and see this person clothed and as the world does. Of course they get this new vantage point of you too, a vantage point that can be fatal to a burgeoning relationship – especially if you're me.

Remarkably though, this was not so with Jamie. When she and I finally step out of the cosy little space we had made for ourselves it feels as though the sanctuary comes with us. When I take her to meet my university friends, the people in my life who helped me enter normality, and so the people whom in many ways I still feel the closest connection to, it's as though she's always been a part of the group, joining in with their ways of gently teasing me, while squeezing my hand tightly under the table to tell me she's really on my side. At brunch with my mother and sister she senses I feel strained and she bolsters me, speaking when I can't find the words, sharing my recent successes she knows I'm too shy to show off about. And when she attends work events with me she displays interest in subjects in which I know she has none and dutifully sits through conversations I'm sure she finds unfathomably boring, that even *I* find unfathomably boring, sits through them with a smile and never once complains.

If that isn't enough, meeting the people in her life also feels easy. Natural. What felt in previous relationships like jumping into unknown waters and struggling against a tide, with Jamie simply feels like walking into a slightly different part of the same pool I've always been standing in. A sunnier, cleaner, nicer part of the pool. Her family are friendly, with apparently no hang-ups about Jamie's sexuality and therefore no hang-ups about me. They are good, honest, hardworking people who don't quite understand Jamie's creativity but admire the fact she's able to make money from it. They seem genuinely glad she's met someone who makes her happy. It makes me feel all types of warm and strange inside to hear they think I make her happy. They're over the moon she's with someone who seems to be in a less precarious career than hers. Clearly they haven't seen the appalling stats on employment prospects within academia, and clearly I have no intention of enlightening them. And her friends seem just like my friends. Or maybe not just like them, maybe not at all like them really, but rather they seem like people I could have been friends with if I'd met them without Jamie. I realise I've never truly had that experience before, the experience of fully enjoying the company of a partner's friends, of seeing a partner's world as anything other than a place I am obliged to endure. Her world is somewhere I might conceivably consider visiting even if she weren't part of it. It is an easy fit for me. It feels right.

The more I get to know of Jamie's world, the more everything I already suspect about her is confirmed. Seeing how the gifts Jamie agonises over light up her friends' and family's faces at Christmas and birthdays shows me the trouble she takes to get to know people, to bring them happiness, and to get things right. Seeing how her friends come to her with their problems, opening up to her, and often to me as an extension of her and as someone provided with her seal of approval, shows me the depth of her understanding, consideration and care. Seeing how she can make even the funniest of her friends crease over with laughter, often through a self-deprecating joke, shows me how absolutely serious her ability to not take herself too seriously is. In other words, Jamie is one of the world's coffee beans. She makes everything around her better, including me, and she appears to ride life's ups and downs with ease, unscathed. Seeing the good humour of her parents, their non-judgemental nature, the warmth in their eyes when they look at each other, and when they look at Jamie and her sisters, I can see how she's become such a perfect little coffee bean, because Jamie, this woman I adore more with each day that passes, has been fashioned out of love and kindness and pride.

I wasn't fashioned out of those things. I made myself out of something entirely different. And although I learned in the first few months with Jamie that I've made something that can withstand close scrutiny, something that does a damn good imitation of normal, eventually I'll always be found out. It's hard to pinpoint when the mask starts to slip, because I want you to understand that I don't ever feel I've been wearing one. I don't ever lie to Jamie or hide anything from her. Rather, Jamie, like most people in love, has chosen to focus on some things and dismiss others.

I think the collage workshop could be the first time Jamie catches a glimpse of something she doesn't like. Jamie's friend Sara is a collage artist, and after perhaps unsurprisingly struggling to make serious money out of the sales of her collages, she has decided to run collage workshops for hen-dos and corporate events. Jamie and her friends are to be her guinea pigs and as the token non-creative in the group, and therefore someone whose opinion may be a truer reflection of the client-base she's aiming for, I have been warmly invited along for the ride.

I must say that Sara does a fine job in a pokey upstairs room of a community centre tucked away on a residential street near Victoria station. She provides snacks, stacks of old magazines, a PowerPoint presentation about famous collage artists everyone in the room seems to already know about, except me. She displays a bubblier personality than I ever remember her sporting before and she asks us to use the materials she's brought, essentially a load of old magazines, to create a picture that represents us, a self-portrait of sorts. We were asked to bring along some of our own magazines too and I happen to have brought a couple of copies of Vice I've had hanging around the flat for a while. Perhaps then it is the raw materials I was working with, but when it comes time for us to view each other's first self-portraits, mine seems to take everyone aback.

As I look around the room I see a lot of bright colours, flowers, and inspirational phrases, and I start to sweat a little from embarrassment at what I have created: an overwhelmingly gloomy portrait of a woman with her mouth gagged and eyes blinded with cut-outs from articles on gang violence and drug abuse. When Jamie, who is sitting across the table from me, sees my piece she looks... arrested. I think that's the right term. She looks at me quizzically and then laughs.

Sara then asks us to destroy the first self-portraits we have made and tells us to use sections of it to create a second piece. Unlike the others in the room, who are more reluctant or even actively opposed to the destruction, I enter into the task with relish. Jamie laughs again when, following more silent absorption in our cutting and pasting and self-expression, she witnesses the resulting second creation, perhaps more grotesque than the first, where I've managed to form what I hope look like tears of blood falling from an already bloodshot eye.

I've worked on making the composition attractive, grotesquely beautiful art is what I'm aiming for, even if it's not what I've achieved. So it is again somewhat disconcerting to see the difference between what I and everyone else has made. Jamie being Jamie, and seeing I feel embarrassed, unconvincingly tells me how much she likes my collage, that she thinks it's terribly good. She just hadn't expected it, that's all, she hadn't known I had it in me. When I reply that I thought everyone had this in them, she just looks at me puzzled and once more brings out that laugh. I am again reminded that I am different, that I don't see things the way other people do, that not everyone has something ugly inside them, that not everyone shares my filter, that my colleagues are not all secretly working to justify suicide as I am, that I am the odd one out. I realise that although I haven't been deliberately hiding, Jamie still hasn't seen me, the real me, yet. But eventually she will.

And of course, she does.

She sees me when I avoid talking in any great detail about my work, becoming irritable when she tries to paint me as a saint to her friends. She sees me when I roll my eyes at therapy evangelists. She sees me when I say that I believe we are who we are, an inextricable blend of our raw ingredients and the method with which we were cooked, and that chatting with a highly-paid stranger isn't going to change that. And of course, she catches glimpses of me in my attitude to my father, an attitude she can pretend to, but can never truly understand. She wants me to either forgive him or stop seeing him, and although the latter is a far more realistic route to push, it's the former she's really backing. And in these conversations, which seem never to end, I see Jamie too. A person who has learned the rules of family from society, from books, from TV, from films, and seen those rules confirmed in her own upbringing. Family loves, family cares, family forgives, family is forever, blood is thicker than water etc. etc. etc. It's difficult, maybe impossible, to ever make a person like Jamie truly understand there are other types of family for whom those general rules not only do not apply but seem like sick jokes. I have never had a need to explain that to Jamie. I don't need or want her to be more like me. That would be tragic. But she wants me to be more like her and more like everyone else. So, the conversation keeps arising.

'Why do you do it to yourself?' she says. 'Why do you not forgive this now harmless old man and enjoy the time you have left together? Why do you torture yourself by visiting him and caring for him when you do not care for him at all?'

I don't know the answers to give that can make her understand without making her live my life from the beginning until now.

And so I say nothing.

And although I use the present tense, as I am wont to do, she doesn't ask me this or anything anymore. Because she doesn't see me anymore, not after finding a fundamental part of me that can't be overlooked. Because if you're Jamie and you've experienced a family that is full of warmth and love, a family that is still around you emanating warmth and love every single day, and you too are full of warmth and love, well, then the fact is that you, Jamie, have too much warmth and love to be contained in just one person. You try to give it to a lover, and they appreciate it, and you are happy together. But there's too much of it for just her alone. You need to give it to more people, and you need to make the world a better place by creating more warm and loving people like yourself.

This is what I come to learn about Jamie.

Yes, Jamie is gay. But no, she, quite rightly, isn't going to let that stop her having children. I learn this about her while she learns it about herself, because when we first meet we are both twenty-five years old, and children are not something we discuss seriously. When the topic arises I say I don't want them and she says she isn't sure. That seems a fine match to me. I make my feelings clear and she seems to accept them. However, once we both hit thirty and some of our friends have already had one, if not two, children, Jamie's position starts to shift. It shifts even further once some of our gay friends start having, or consider having, children. These friends are usually slightly older, living as we all tend to do on a queer timeline generally delayed as compared to that of straights, and their IVF tales bring out something in Jamie I hadn't seen before.

It emerges Jamie had always assumed she would have children, or so she says, and she had also assumed that as I aged I would change my mind. Which can hardly be pinned on me as my fault, right? Yet I feel like it is, because maybe any other normal person would have changed their mind, but here I am wasting her time. Her ovaries are getting their internal equivalent of the grey hair and wrinkles starting to appear on our bodies, and they won't hold on forever. She tries to scare me out of something she hopes is simply immaturity by showing me fertility graphs she finds online depicting steep drops in female fertility post age thirty-five. She tries to help me reflect upon my reluctance to start a family as being a common and entirely reasonable but changeable response to a lack of queer-family role models. She tries to suggest my discomfort with the concept of creating new life could be linked to possible gender-dysphoria over being a *mother*, and she tries to encourage me to imagine instead being simply a *parent*. And I try to hear her. I try to open my mind. I try to show her I respect her arguments. There's certainly some truth to them. Without a blueprint to follow it can be difficult to muster the confidence to build a queer family in what will inevitably be a sometimes hostile environment. And personally I can't imagine doing anything more disturbingly feminine than carrying a child: it would be like being forced to

86

wear a frilly bridesmaid dress and heels, but inside my bloody womb, for nine full months.

It's just not me.

But they're not my reasons.

Or certainly not my only or main reasons.

I try to explain to Jamie that if I were to ever have children I would want them to be hers, but that I wouldn't be any good as a parent. That I have bad genes and bad environmental experiences I don't want to pass on, that it wouldn't be fair to pass on, and that she couldn't handle bringing up someone with my input. I try to explain to her that the last thing I want is to become my father to someone, and that I would do anything to prevent it. I try to explain to her that no child deserves me. And I think I get through to her. Because after more than a year of these conversations she accepts that I won't be changing my mind. She decides she's ok with that, because although she wants a child, she wants me more.

Huzzah, right? I'm the winner. I win.

But if I win, that means Jamie loses, and her unborn children and the rest of the world lose too. Because the world needs more people like her, more life-improving coffee beans, and she would make a fucking fantastic mother. I don't want to be the person to take that from her.

What can I do but end it? My hand is forced.

So I continue to visit my dad, and when I come home I sit alone in my koala pyjamas and eat cereal for dinner, and there is no one here to ask me why I do this to myself except me.

A BLACK DAY

Jamie's pitched it just right. She looks beautiful, but not too beautiful, holding a flower arrangement that's elegant, but not too elegant. Well done Jamie.

I usually register her presence as soon as she arrives in a place. I sort of sense her. It's like she changes the very air of any room she enters. Is it her smell? Her pheromones? The reaction she provokes in others? Whatever it is, somehow something usually feels softer when she's near.

She's near now. She's here for me. She's showing her support. Today I see it. Jamie's presence. Jamie's support. But I don't feel it. I process it cognitively. That's nice of her to bring flowers, I think. But it doesn't feel nice. Nothing feels nice.

A BROTHER

As children, my brother Rob and I used to be playmates and, I would say, good friends. He's four years younger than I and although I used to play tricks on him and tickle him and wind him up whenever I got the chance, I was also a fiercely protective older sister. I once knocked a boy's tooth out for Rob. Said boy was a year older than me and when I heard he was bullying my brother I saw red. I found the bully laughing with some friends in a nearby park and I went for him. I didn't mean to knock his tooth out of course. I was simply telling him to stop the cowardly bullying of a boy five years his junior. I was also pushing him a little, to emphasise my point and how serious I was about it. Then, after a particularly forceful push, he fell over a bike that was on the floor, smacked his face on the handlebar and ran away crying, bloody, and with one less tooth in his head. It seemed my point had been made. I hadn't intended to cause such permanent damage but I'd have taken on him and all his friends too to make them leave Rob alone.

When I look back on our childhood together, before I became a moody teenager and before our little sister came along, it's a blur of sunshine and sweat and ice pops and tree-climbing and water-fighting and den-building and make believe. I know it can't have always been that way, I know we used to fight, and we live in England after all, so there can't have been that much bloody sunshine. But that's how it feels, that time with him.

One summer's day from our childhood stands out in particular. I'm nine and Rob is five. It must be a weekend because our parents are both home and my dad has spent all day screaming at my mum. This isn't an unusual occurrence but on this particular day it seems especially loud, making it rather difficult for us to concentrate on any of our games. How can we be Power Rangers saving the world from Rita Repulsa and Lord Zedd when our dad is raging and our mum is crying? As director of our games I am trying my best, but it just doesn't make narrative sense. Ever resourceful, I decide to switch the role-play to something that can incorporate the fighting. We are no longer Power Rangers and instead we are the unfortunate offspring of a violent and unhappy marriage. I congratulate myself on my phenomenal imagination. The new game sees us dealing with our lot in life by hatching a plan to run away from home. Planning is a serious business and we spend a great deal of time strategising, drawing our escape route and compiling a list of the items we'll need to take with us. Once this is done we set about collecting said items, or as close to said items as we can manage. A piece of string we never have a use for that lives in the bottom kitchen drawer becomes a length of rope. A half-eaten packet of glucose tablets and some Sesame Snaps found in the same drawer become a month's supply of freeze-dried astronaut food to tide us through the leaner times. We fill a backpack with this loot for what promises to be a gruelling and treacherous trip. We plan to cycle to a nearby woodland and build our lives as wood children there. If we get bored of that wood, or if we hear from other wood children we befriend about better woods, then we will move on. Wherever we lay our Teenage Mutant Ninja Turtles baseball caps will be our home.

There is a wood we have been to before with our cousins, but of course neither of us knows how to get there again without a car and our aunt to drive us. That isn't a problem though, because we do know how to get to the corner shop where we always buy our penny sweets, so we plan to cycle there to ask Mr P for directions, as well as picking up some essential sustenance for woodland living in the form of sour gobstoppers and fizzy cola bottles for me – I have long suspected my grommets and adenoid removal as a child left me with an impaired sense of taste and a hankering for flavours that make others' eyes water – and foam bananas for my brother, who has more pedestrian tastes and his adenoids intact. Mr P will surely know the way, and if we palm him a few extra pennies we trust he'll keep his mouth shut about seeing us, and of course destroy the CCTV evidence before the police arrive.

When a lull in the shouting lasts long enough for us to feel safe, and when neither parent is anywhere near the doors, we teeter off to find our new lives. We leave through the open back door so as not to draw attention but as soon as we turn into the alley we understand why things have gone so quiet inside. Sitting against the wall, knees pulled up to her chin, is our mum.

We've been caught, we're done for, our perfect plan is foiled.

Except then I realise her head is downturned and she is so absorbed in crying that she seems utterly oblivious to our presence. Even if she sees us, I reassure myself, she doesn't know of our top-secret super-duper plan to become woodland children. For all she knows we are just playing our usual games. I whisper to my brother to just act naturally and I try to take this advice myself. I pedal past her and then speed up, turning into the street with Rob close behind. I race up the street, my brother working double time to keep up with me. I keep turning back to see if my mum, or even worse my dad – please don't be my dad – is running after us, but they aren't. I turn left at the top of the road and screech to a halt, nearly sending my brother flying as he turns left after me.

'Come on, let's go before they come after us,' he says, confused about why we are muddying such an apparently clean getaway.

I peek around the corner, certain I'll see them coming up the road after us by now.

But there is nothing.

'We have to go back,' I declare after it becomes totally clear no one's following us. The image won't leave me; my mum crying in her nightie, sitting on the dirty ground, the same ground where she shouts at us for playing with woodlice and ants and worms. We have to go back and be with her. We are her children and she needs us. Helping her should be our new mission. Plus, it's dawning on me that I haven't brought a warm enough coat and that I don't actually really fancy sleeping in a wood and that there are probably more likely to be weird wood men than wonderful wood children in the woods and that my stomach is starting to rumble and I want something for dinner other than sweets.

'We have to be there for Mum.'

'No. Please,' Rob says.

He doesn't understand why we're giving up our head start, or why seeing our mum there crying changes anything. I try to explain, but only in the most perfunctory and dismissive way, knowing there is no need to convince him, knowing I am the boss of these games and where I go, he will follow. I cycle back with my brother cycling next to me pleading with me to turn around. It seems the quiet wasn't a lull, the fighting has finished for the day. Rob doesn't speak to me all evening and he goes to bed early. When I walk past his room I could swear I hear him crying.

The next day all is well and we resume our friendship by knocking for Nicholas who lives four doors down and asking if we can have a dip in his paddling pool and play dress-up with the collection of his mum's old cast-off costume jewellery which Rob and I love and think is the height of luxury and sophistication.

We never speak of that day and our abandoned plan again. I didn't give any of it much thought until years later. But I look back on that event now as one of significance. A symbol. Upon reflection I realise Rob was too young to understand we were never going to be wood children, that the game was just that, a game, that the plan was make-believe and the characters we were playing, the children who were brave enough to leave their suffering behind in search of something more, who were strong enough to build something happy together, they were make believe too. I now think Rob was indeed crying that evening, as I would have been too, if I had ever truly thought, if I had ever been led to believe by someone I trusted and looked up to, that we could be something more than we were destined to be and then been so rudely awoken from that dream.

I don't know whether Rob even remembers this incident. I could ask him, but we don't talk anymore, not about anything important anyway. When I visit my mum's house, where Rob, now thirty-one, still lives, he tries to hide from me. I don't take it personally because I think he probably tries to hide from everyone and everything. He grows his beard and hair long and wears thick-rimmed glasses. Outsiders interpret Rob's look as hip, and it is, but I see it as an attempt to put distance between himself and the world, building barriers to hide behind. He spends most of his time in his room, the threshold of which appears to be some sort of uncharted gap in the space-time continuum, opening as it does from my mum's rather cluttered and messy, yet still relatively mundane, suburban house directly into a drug den. Rob's mattress is on the floor surrounded by cigarette butts, rolling papers, and those little metal laughing gas bulbs you see littering the streets. But there isn't much laughter in the air.

Resting against the wall in one corner of the room is an untouched guitar my parents bought Rob when he thought he'd be a musician. Next to it, the barely used decks from his incredibly short DJ-phase lie under a box of paints from the day or two he pretended he might try to do some art. He's got hard-capped boots gathering dust, boots given to him by a neighbour who hoped he might help on a building site one day. He never did. And there's a scratched and broken desk in one corner which perhaps once served its intended purpose as a workspace, possibly during his fleeting poetry or start-up or web-designer stage, but if it did it was long ago. Now it acts as a podium displaying all my brother has actually produced in his life, empty beer cans, marijuana debris, and takeaway wrappers. Despite this hovel, on the few occasions Rob does venture outside, there seem to be no end of women – attractive, eligible women – unable to resist his big baby-blue eyes, dirty-blonde curls, and taciturn manner. I've even happened to see a couple of these women sneak out of his room over the years, apparently and mind-bogglingly not minding the mess. They want to look after Rob, I think, want to help him open up, but he never lets them, going through women as quickly as he does six-packs of beer. Maybe I made that sound fun, but Rob never appears to enjoy himself much at all.

When I visit my mum, as I have today, Rob doesn't usually feature in the visit. I sit in the living room, oppressively surrounded by my mum's aforementioned clutter. Behind us there are three flowery armchairs stacked on top of an even more flowery sofa, all hailing from a clear-out of my grandma's house after she passed away ten years ago. The furniture looms over us like a garish upholstery garden as we sip tea on one of the three usable sofas in a room barely big enough for one. Two of these sofas arrived after a clear-out of my aunt's house when she moved abroad twenty years ago and were outdated in their design even then. When I want to put my mug down I ponder which of the two coffee tables in front of us – one from my aunt, one I think actually bought by my mum herself – to use. I opt instead to place it on the nested side table to my right, which, if I remember correctly, was a neighbour's cast-off. It makes a reasonable partner to the two side tables wedged next to my mum, but they all clash with the one inherited from my Grandma in the corner of the room. Jamie used to say she loved it in here. I would tease that she only loved it because she viewed the house as a piece of *waste not-want not* performance art. This would make her feel guilty, until I kissed her forehead and told her I was only joking and that I loved that she loved this unlovable house. Because I'd be too ashamed to invite most people over, even though I don't notice the clutter myself anymore. I know it can be overwhelming, all these ways of living piled on top of each other. But the trick is not to see any of it, to only see the gaps through which it's possible to move. Then it's, if not lovable, at least liveable.

My mum's telling me about her latest visit to the GP. She's one of the GP's frequent flyers, the stress she suffered at the hands of my dad, in my opinion, resulting in her acquiring her very own auto-immune disease, rheumatoid arthritis. Her knuckles are swollen, her hands and feet misshapen, because her body has been attacking her own joints. Joints being fairly important for moving and living, the disease isn't much fun. She becomes irate about the latest time the GP has slighted her. He really is a terrible GP but she refuses to switch even though there are multiple practices closer by, an unfortunate habit of hers, sticking with awful people for too long. Above me on the landing, and then the stairs, then behind me in the hall, and then to the left of me in the kitchen, I think I hear my brother scuttling about like a rat. Remember they're more scared of you than you are of them, I think. I'm not sure that's the case with rats though, is it? Maybe that's a saying for spiders? But either way, I suspect it's true of Rob. If I ever do encounter him his arrogance is almost as overpowering as the cannabis smell wafting from him. He doesn't say hello unless I do and even then it's 50:50 odds on whether he'll reply, and any attempt at further conversation is batted away like a pesky fly.

It's tempting to regress to our childhood dynamics, to slap him around the head and run and tell Mum about his rudeness, but I remind myself that no one happy with themselves acts like Rob. No one confident enough to verge on true arrogance lives the way Rob lives. This is backed up by the anti-depressant packets that occasionally – far too occasionally – accompany the self-medication waste in his pit. So, I don't slap him around the head and I don't bring his rudeness into the room as a topic for discussion. I simply shrug it off as if it's nothing. And it often feels like nothing. It's just him. It felt like something fifteen years ago when it started, it felt heart-breaking. Now it's simply the Rob I'm used to, just the man he is.

Today, as I sit with my mum, I entertain the idea of ambushing Rob in the kitchen, telling him he can't get away that easily, that he should say hello to his big sister. But for some reason I don't think I can handle his inevitable dismissiveness right now. I wish we really and truly could regress. Not just so I could slap him around his stupid head. I wish we could be the people we were twenty-five years ago, I wish we could remember, even for just one conversation, how close we had been. How he'd been my sidekick and I, his protector. I could tell him I still remember exactly what his small sticky chubby hand felt like in mine, walking to the corner shop, helping him over a gate, picking him up when he fell. I can remember his hands so much more clearly than I can remember my own, the purple birthmark on his right hand where the skin was always a little thicker and harder than that surrounding it, the nails always bitten down until they bled. I could ask him if he thinks siblings ever hold hands as adults and if he thinks he and I will ever hold hands again. It seems like an impossible, almost obscene thing to do, to hold his hand. And I would tell him how sad that makes me. I would ask if he remembers the time I knocked a bully's tooth out for him. And I would apologise for not saving him from the worst bully in his life, the bully that has defined him and all of us. I would apologise for not running away with him and for never even intending to run away with him. I would apologise for letting him believe there could be something better. Because maybe that's why he is where he is, and I am where I am. I always knew there was no one who could protect me and magically make everything right. I always accepted my world exactly as it was. That sounds depressing, and maybe it is, but acceptance meant I made the best of it – I had no other choice. I looked only for the gaps through which it was possible to move, and I used them. But maybe I was part of letting Rob believe that people have protectors, that the bullies can be stopped, that he would be saved. Maybe he's still holed up in his room 24-7 waiting for someone to fix everything.

But I'm being self-pitying and morose. None of that bullshit matters. So, even if I did corner him in the kitchen and force him to speak to me, to look at me, which I won't, I wouldn't say any of that. I don't know why I turned out semi-functioning after our upbringing, and Rob can barely function at all. I just know I'm the anomalous one. I'm the lucky one who escaped the warzone with nothing but some itchy skin and a cold heart. Rob's injuries are far more typical in casualties of this particular type of battle. The way I see it, there was only one thing I could have done to help prevent them. I could have let the worst thing that ever happened to us die when I had the chance. So, maybe I could apologise for not doing what I could back then?

But it's not that simple.

A BLACK DAY

I can't remember the last time I saw Rob in a suit. Maybe at Freya's graduation? I wonder how old the suit is. From the way it fits, I'm guessing pretty old. It's probably a suit he was bought as a teenager, maybe for someone's wedding, or for his sixth-form prom, or for job interviews my parents hoped would materialise. It's not that it's too small that's the giveaway. It's that it is too big. Like something bought with growth in mind, growth that never came. He looks good all the same. He looks smart.

He wasn't nervous about speaking in front of all these people and it seems he had no need to be. When it's his turn he speaks the words he has written loudly, calmly, slowly, clearly. They are blunt words, and they are all the more moving for it.

'...always told good stories...can't believe it...wish I could change it... I should have been more helpful...'

I thought I'd already broken as much as I possibly could, but his words find a new piece of me to smash.

A SISTER

My parents divorced when I was twenty-four. It was a surreal experience, something I hadn't thought could actually happen, something in truth I hadn't ever dared dream about. But my mum got there. She battled through. She lost a lot of money, weight, and time in the drawn-out two-year process, and with my dad resisting in every way he could, it was an utterly awful experience that felt endless. But she got there. *Why didn't she do it earlier?* I hear the untouched-by-abuse cry. As violent and drunken and despicable as my father was when they divorced, he was far more unhinged, and frankly, far more energetic in his violence, as a younger man. She never stopped fearing he would murder her and her children for leaving him, but in her cost-benefit analysis she felt the probability had decreased significantly with age. Even with the risk lowered, if she hadn't been financially independent and successful in her own career, and pretty bloody smart to boot, there is no way she could have managed it. I don't know how stay-at-home victims of abuse ever get out. I imagine fewer do, but for those who manage it, we should help in every way we can, because they have more bravery, grit, and determination than anyone else.

By the time of the divorce I was twenty-four and had been living outside of the family home and avoiding it as much as possible for six years. Yet still the impact of the separation was tremendous. I could visit my mum, who is a homebody at heart, without terror. I could go home for Christmas without the knowledge that I would more than likely lose rather than gain sleep over my *relaxing* festive break from work. And I could go back to work afterwards and not lie completely about what had happened out of shame. I could unclench. Not entirely, as my dad still made impromptu drunken aggressive visits every now and again, despite the restraining order. But I could relax somewhat. And that was a revelation.

It still strikes me as strange how people react to the news of divorce. I have to remind myself that we can only react based on our own knowledge and experiences, and because of my knowledge and experiences, I am still surprised when people look sad and sympathetic. When they bow their heads and offer their condolences. My mum's colleagues, when they first found out, would stroke her hand and softly ask how the children were taking the news. When she told me this I had exactly the same reaction as she did – I nearly wet myself laughing. When I receive the sympathy eyes upon sharing my parents' marital status, I try to explain to people that there are some offspring, probably many, many offspring, whose greatest wish is that their parents divorce. It always falls flat. Perhaps it seems like I'm overcompensating to hide my true sadness? It must be difficult for those from a semi-happy family to understand, but some parents' divorces leave no trace of misery in their children. They mark an end to misery.

I can only imagine what that feeling might have been like if it had happened while I was still growing up. I hypothesise that the fewer formative years I spent in my father's close quarters, the more well-developed and normal I would have been. But perhaps I've got my working wrong, because that's not how it's happened for my sister, Freya. She's the complication that messes up what could have been a pure and simple biggest-regret-of-my-life type deal. The baby of the family, she is a full ten years younger than I am. So she came along quite some time *after* I stopped my dad from topping himself. No Dad equals no Dad's sperm equals no Freya. Tricky.

Freya was freed at fourteen, parental divorce-wise. She felt the same relief as I did, the same permanent exhale of long-held breath. But it doesn't seem to have done her much good. Now, don't get me wrong, Freya's no Rob. She manages to function and stand on her own two feet. Sort-of. She manages to communicate with others in words rather than grunts. But she's hanging on by a thread. Or by a pill, or a powder, or a drink. She keeps herself afloat through a combination of credit card debts, *loans* from our mum, and flitting from temping job to temping job, leaving just as the employers wake up to the fact she's been doing little more than temporarily using their lavatories as a place to sleep off a heavy night.

Today Freya has invited me to a club night where her friend is DJing. Being thirty-five, and in truth long having had the stamina of a woman of fifty-five, I am extremely flattered to be considered young and fun enough to attend. Of course her invitation probably indicates she's running low on cash and wants big sis' to pay for drinks, but still, I have to take what I'm given with Freya.

We arrive at the club and we buy — I buy — two-for-one Espresso Martinis. Freya looks radiant, having spent the whole day preening for this night. I've come directly from a day in the lab and I look like it, needing the coffee shot in my sickly sweet drink more than I need the alcohol. We sit in a corner of the rather hip and overly dark club and start by sharing boring work catchups, and then move on to revel in our childhood memories. Or maybe it's more correct to say that I revel in our childhood memories, because most of what is being recounted is by me and involves a Freya too young to know what was going on. She can't remember, for instance, that I used to take her to school and pick her up for many years before I left for university. She simply has no recollection of it. It's become a running joke between us, Freya accuses me of lying about it, of trying to take credit for something I never did. She throws her head back and laughs at my mock frustration. It's a familiar routine which works especially well if we are with a crowd of her companions. But my part in the routine is a double bluff. Because I *am* frustrated, and I am hurt. I walked her to school and picked her up every day, often making myself late for school in the morning, and having to turn down invitations of fun in the evening. I changed her nappies, I sat in her playpen with her, I built snow animals with her and rubbed her hands when they got so cold she cried. I was a school child alongside her stuffed toys when she wanted to be a teacher, I was a customer hungry for crisps when she wanted to run a shop, I was the hand she held in the night when my dad wasn't letting anyone sleep, I was the big sister she was proud to have collect her from parties. These memories mean something to me, but Freya barely remembers a thing. It feels so unbalanced that sometimes when she's teasing me for *lying* about these things and I'm shaking my head and sticking out my lower lip in a parody of pain, my chest hurts. And sometimes I feel like she's right and maybe none of it really happened at all, or it might as well not have done, it might as well have been a different little girl, so far-removed is she from this person in front of me now. Is this how parents feel? Or is it because I left home when she was still young that her memories of me went too?

Anyway, we are at this club night and we are running through the old routine and my chest is hurting a little and as the empty cocktail glasses stack up Freya is on fine form, beaming at me and making me feel special, and wanted even, as she looks around the room for the people she's expecting to arrive soon. She's making fun of me yet making me laugh, making me glad to be here in her company, and when we are finally joined by others Freya's light grows, and she wears the self-assured face she always wears when she's drunk and socialising, like she's the happiest person in the room. She is positively glowing and her flame attracts people to us. I try my best to reflect some of her light as she introduces me to a long line of colleagues from her latest job, which is where she met the DJ, who is also an office temp by day. I can see how proud she is and with each introduction she beams more widely as though the more people one knows, the more valuable one is. But her shine doesn't stop me from realising that I have never met anyone more than once through Freya. I've often felt that if she had her way, and she almost entirely does, she would never see the same people twice, content with shining bright for one night only and moving on.

When Freya went travelling across Asia and Australia after university I was in awe of her; this new graduate, this young woman, this baby of the family, heading off all on her own to the other side of the world to have adventures. I told and still tell myself that of course I could go travelling – and certainly on a short holiday – alone, I simply don't want to. But I wasn't sure that was the truth back then, and I'm even less certain now. So, to me her feat was incredible, evidence my little sister had grown into her own woman, a better and more courageous woman than I was or might ever be, and that filled me with pride at any part I'd played in moulding her. The warmth of that pride didn't stop me puzzling at her tales when she returned though, because the thing she raved about most, apart from the dangerous levels of mind-altering substances and sun exposure she had enjoyed, was how much she loved spending only a few days in each place. She was ebullient as she recalled ditching person after person while they still seemed exciting, sharing how she loved being able to play a character for a few days before shedding that identity for the next, with no one any the wiser. She couldn't understand why this didn't make me down tools and set off on my own travels immediately and I couldn't understand why she needed to *play* anyone other than herself. I put it down to age – don't we all experiment with different identities in our youth? Weren't we all the more desperate to please and be accepted? But Freya hasn't grown out of this particular trait. She still loves making a bloody good first impression and then moving on. My mum, brother, and I are perhaps Freya's only constants, or the only ones I know of. And I always get the sense she wants rid of us too. She wants only people who see her like she is right here right now in this club. People who only see her floating like an inebriated angel, people who only see the surface, they see her and they can't help but smile. My chest hurts more when I think this, because even as she stands right next to me, smiling at me as we share a wonderful evening, she also always feels so close to an open door, rootless, ready to leave at any time, and I don't want her to leave.

In a rare moment of quiet when it is just the two of us at the table, presumably because everyone else is either on the dancefloor or in the toilet or at the bar or in the smoking area, Freya turns my attention away from her and she asks me about Jamie. She tells me she doesn't know why but she feels she has to be very, very, veerrrryyy honest right now. I tell her it's probably because of all the vodka and kalua. She tells me I am the worst and to shut up and listen because she has something to say. She tells me she feels she can say this to me now that it's been a while, of course she didn't feel she could say anything at first, considering the situation, but she thinks it's surely been long enough now that she can finally speak her mind on something. She tells me she misses Jamie terribly and has done ever since we ended. I seem to also be feeling rather honest – drunk – because I tell her, albeit in a jovial way, that it's not really her place to miss Jamie, and that even if she does find herself missing Jamie, despite, as mentioned, it not at all being her place to miss Jamie, she probably shouldn't tell me about it. But Freya persists, saying she has to get this off her chest, and it's time I heard this, and she goes on to tell me about all the individual things she misses about Jamie, apparently unwittingly in alphabetical order. She starts with *accent*.

'Jamie had such a great voice didn't she? Where was it from again, that accent? Or was it accent*less*, perhaps that's why I liked it so much? And god, how she dressed, her attire was amazing. I always meant to ask her where she got those trousers from, y'know? The black ones that were kind of smart but also, like, really relaxed? Actually, do you know where they were from?'

I don't answer, I'm just staring at her, and then she moves on to b for breasts.

'Not being funny, but she had great tits didn't she? Not like your other exes who've all been more, like, straight up and down. So, are you more into boobs now?'

I try to think of ways to stop her talking. Maybe it would help if I tell her how even the mention of Jamie's name still makes me wince in pain? I think it probably would. But I don't say that, because despite the copious amounts of alcohol I've consumed, I find it especially hard to be open about my emotions when I've just been punched in the stomach by sadness. I just listen on, trying to keep a neutral face as we progress through the alphabet and misery floods my body. We get to what I suppose must be *interpreter*, coming as it does after *interesting*.

'She was really chill, but, like, never boring chill. She always had something clever to say about stuff that would, like, make you think, didn't she?' Freya leans her head back and appraises me, then continues. 'She definitely had beautiful tits, but I think I miss the effect she had on you the most. You're not the same without her. Or maybe you are the same, but your same was better then. Jamie made all of this...' here she waves her unsteady hand to indicate all of me, '...make sense. You made sense with her, you were more...more...'

My chest nearly breaks open as I look into her doe eyes and realise, fully properly realise, that Freya isn't simply being a mindless, selfish, drunken mess right now. That she means all of this, and that it's actually intended for my benefit. It dawns on me that our pity is two-way. That those two people, those children, whom at least *I* remember playing in the snow and reading to one another all those years ago, are now sitting here drunk in a bar feeling sorry for one another – are perhaps *only* in this bar together in the first place because they feel sorry for one another.

Why should I feel sorry for Freya, you might ask? Maybe she has the right idea? She's living a life many would admire. The glamourous party girl, the mysterious wanderer, even if she isn't often wandering far. Sometimes I think she's got life sussed, especially on nights like this where she seems so full of sparkle, so up, so high. But then there are the other times.

Two days after the night in the club I'm at my dad's apartment when I receive a missed call from Freya. I'm cooking while imagining hitting him over the head with the frying pan. I tell people I don't like being constantly contactable, which is true, but also no one really contacts me anyway, so my phone is on silent mode in my bag. This means I don't notice the missed call until I'm almost ready to leave. Freya has left a voicemail, which strikes me as odd because she knows I have a personal policy to disregard all voicemails. I'm trying to ignore the trepidation building in my stomach. She wouldn't do it again, right? And she wouldn't call me if she did? Someone else would call me, like they always do. I listen to it, begrudgingly, once I've taken a seat on the bus, expecting to find either a couple of seconds of accidental dead air or a cackling Freya revelling in the fact she's duped me into listening to a blasted voicemail. There is no dead air on the voicemail. Instead there's an almost unintelligible and hysterical voice. I jump off the bus and into a cab to the latest place Freya shares with a bunch of strangers. I keep my finger on the doorbell until one of them – the Spanish one, or perhaps Portuguese? – lets me in. I run up to Freya's box room and find it empty, so I barge into every other room on that floor until I eventually find her in the bathroom slumped over a toilet filled with vomit, that upon frantic inspection I see is mostly bile and half-digested pills. After I make her promise me the pills in the toilet account for most if not all of those she took, I explode. I am livid and wanting a target at which to hurl my fury. How had her housemates not noticed this? They most certainly know about her diagnosis. She's very open about it. Why hadn't they been watching out for her? This is why Freya should live with people who actually give at least a single shit about her. These arseholes don't care about anyone but themselves. I say all of this out loud. Repeatedly. With more expletives. Hoping said housemates can hear me as I become dizzy from pacing the tiny bathroom – filling these strangers with the hate I feel for this action, *her* action.

Freya raises her head up from the toilet seat and groggily tells me I shouldn't be mad at them; she'd been in her room the whole day so they'd probably assumed she was just hungover, and indeed she reckons she probably was just hungover and feeling rotten and took it too far. I try to be firm, but Freya insists she doesn't want her stomach pumped again, and she doesn't want to visit a doctor, that she simply felt low and had done something silly, but she had changed her mind immediately and hardly anything could have gone in. I sit on the grubby bathroom carpet – yes, carpet in the bathroom, lovely place – stroking her hair while she cries into the toilet bowl, pulling her away from it for long enough to flush most of the pungent smell away and then letting her head loll back onto the seat. She promises me she is still taking her medication and that she will tell her psychiatrist what happened when she sees her next week and that she only ever feels like this on a comedown anyway. I try to tell her, again, that comedowns are why it's not worth taking drugs, or not those kinds of drugs anyway, if you're someone like her. *Sensitive.* But she just rolls her eyes at me like she always does. And I don't blame her, the big sister routine must get pretty bloody boring for her, but unfortunately I can't turn it off.

When she asks where I was when she called, I tell her I was cooking dinner at Dad's. She looks up at me and tells me she always forgets I still do that, that she can't remember the last time she saw him, and isn't it funny how I'm the one who always hated him the most yet I'm the one who sees him the most? She laughs about this, a horrible raspy laugh, and then cries some more. When she tires herself out with crying she lets me take her to bed and help her drink some water. After staying up with her for most of the night and inspecting the empty pill packets for comparison with what I'd seen in the bowl, I am finally suitably convinced she isn't going to drop dead any minute and she probably hasn't damaged her liver irreparably. I crawl into bed behind her and spoon her. We rock back and forth until she eventually lets herself sleep, and then so do I.

When I wake the next morning, late for work, it's like emerging into another universe. It takes me a while to remember where I am and through sleep-bleared eyes I can see a croissant and orange juice on the bedside table along with a note that reads: *Sorry about last night, I was a bit of a mess! Off to work now, feel free to eat anything in the fridge, Ursula and Marta won't mind! *Smiley face* *Kiss kiss kiss*.*

So, that's Freya.

A SHOULDER

But that's unfair. That's not all of Freya. It's a big part of her. But she could always be a lot more than that.

It's years ago now. It's the day I leave Jamie. I'm standing over her in the living room. Jamie. I know I've just said words I've been rehearsing for weeks, but blood was pumping so loudly in my ears I couldn't hear myself speak, and I can't recall now if the words were coherent. I know she is and has been begging and crying. There is still so much crying. Coherent or not, I guess I must have conveyed my message. I can't stand to see Jamie in pain. I would murder anyone who hurt her with my bare fucking hands. And that's not just an expression, I really would. But I did this. I've hurt her more than I ever thought she could be hurt. I want to murder myself. I think I hit myself in the face, but I don't feel it, and Jamie is crumpled on the floor in front of me, crying with her head down, so she doesn't see it. Maybe I imagined it. I imagine doing worse. I want to beat the living shit out of myself. I don't think I would feel it though, not right now. I'm numb.

On autopilot I walk to our bedroom – to *her* bedroom – and pick up the bag I've packed. I'll return for the rest of my things later. I walk to the front door and I leave without looking back. When I get to the tube station I notice people looking at me strangely, and I realise it's because I'm repeating 'I'm sorry. You'll be fine' over and over. I think maybe I've been repeating this the whole time. I don't stop. I can still hear Jamie crying, and I wonder if she's followed me. But she's just in my head. That's the only place I'll see or hear her now.

As I let myself into my flat it finally hits me: what I've done, what I've lost, what I've given away, and I crash to the floor under the weight of it all. I'm sitting in the entrance with the door still open, rocking backwards and forwards, hugging my bag to my chest. I know I deserve to feel this pain, but it's too much to bear. I can't breathe for crying. I can't think. I sit here for hours. The pain is made worse because I know I could stop it – my pain and Jamie's pain – if I just turn around and go back. But that wouldn't be fair. I remind myself my decision is made. I remind myself I've done the right thing. My phone has been ringing non-stop. Jamie. I delete her number from my phone without even writing it down because I can't trust my future self to be strong in the face of this agony. Jamie's number, with no name now, keeps calling. I see it on the screen and realise I know it off by heart. I want to tear off all my skin. I sit here for hours. I can't see any windows, and yet somehow I know it must have become dark.

Then I can feel it's become light again. I'm still here, in the doorway. Have I been here all night? Shouldn't I be hungry? I hear people moving in the other flats. I realise what I must look like. I don't want anyone to see me. I crawl inside and close the door. I lie in the hallway and sleep. But only for a few hours. Then I just lie. My phone is still buzzing, the light constantly on. And then it's off. I think it must have died. I want to die. I'm surprised the battery lasted this long. How long has it been? How long will *my* battery last? I should eat. I find a cereal bar in my coat pocket. I unwrap it and raise it to my mouth, but the smell makes me feel sick, so I wrap it up again and put it back. At least I know it's there. I drift here for what feels like a long time. I think it's become dark and light again. I just lie here. The hardwood floor hurts my cheek, but I stay here until I can't feel it anymore. I want to melt into it. I think maybe it's starting to happen. My eyes have become too swollen and dry to continue crying so I just stare at the wall underneath my radiator. The skirting board is dusty. I imagine the dust entering my nose as I breathe, furring my nasal passage, collecting in my lungs. It makes me want to vomit. It makes me want to die. I move in and out of sleep seamlessly, I'm never sure which state I'm in.

Then a knock and I'm definitely awake. Someone is at my door, pounding. I don't think I can take it if it's Jamie. What's left of my heart would shatter if she were here. So I don't move. I ignore it. The knock comes again. Harder. Then there's a voice and my heart shatters anyway, precisely because it's *not* Jamie. It's Freya. I still ignore it. I have nothing to give Freya right now. I want to disappear. I'm sure she'll go soon. She doesn't. I try to focus on her words. What is she saying? I think she's saying Jamie's name. I zone in harder. She knows about what happened. She called Jamie. Why did she call Jamie? Her voice moves lower somehow. Closer. Is she sitting? On the other side of the door? She tried to call me, she says. She was feeling down. Of course. Again. But then I didn't answer and she got worried. So she called Jamie. Why didn't I tell her what was going on? She says she'll wait here for me, she's not going anywhere. She stops talking but I know she's still there. I can feel her. I stay looking at the wall underneath the radiator.

I think the light has changed again, I'm not sure how many times. We're silent, but I know Freya's still there. Her presence doesn't make me feel better, but it doesn't make me feel worse. Eventually I get up because I need the loo. Why haven't I needed it before? Have I soiled myself without realising it? I don't know, but either way the movement helps me realise I do not smell good. I use the toilet and Freya must hear me because she's saying she knew I was in, and she's asking me to please open the door. I do. Her look of shock and sadness slaps me in the face. I crumple again, this time into her arms. She half carries me to my bed. I haven't stayed here for so long it doesn't have any bedding on it. Jamie's place has been my home for years and this flat has belonged more to my various short-term lodgers than to me. Thankfully they're all gone now, so they don't have to witness this, but it takes me a moment to remember where I keep the bedding. When I do, Freya sits me in a nearby chair and I watch her wrestle with the fitted sheet and duvet cover. She's very slow and bad at it, but she gets there in the end, and then she helps me in. She points to my face and asks if Jamie did this. I touch my cheek and it hurts. I shake my head. I did it all. Apart from that, she doesn't make me talk. Which is good because I don't think I could. She just brings me things and calls me *Silly Jess* and strokes my forehead, which feels nice. When she stops stroking I ask her to start again, and she does. She makes me eat and drink. Drinking is easy, I'm so thirsty. Eating is much harder. Everything makes me wretch. She persists though, bringing me plain boiled rice and forcing me to have at least a few spoonfuls.

Days pass. It occurs to me I have a job I have abandoned. Freya tells me she's sorted it. She called and told them she was treating me to a surprise birthday treat holiday, even though it's nowhere near my birthday. Presumably that heightened the surprise. A few days later and it occurs to me Freya also has a job, a temp job at least. She's sorted that too. Apparently she's also been taken on an oddly-timed surprise birthday trip. She told them it was by a tall hot muscley guy though, not her lame older sister. I laugh. It feels nice.

When I'm feeling well enough to eat a full bowl of rice, Freya brings the TV into my room and crawls into bed next to me. We spend days having movie marathons. I thank her. Then I cry. She tells me it will get easier. I tell her I bloody hope so. If I thought it would always feel this way I would have killed myself by now. I laugh. She doesn't. She looks concerned, so I tell her I was only joking. I'm not sure if that's true. This is terrible. But it would be even worse without Freya here.

In these ways Freya gradually picks me up. She feeds me more and more each day, ensuring my body doesn't simply vanish, as I hope it will. She watches films with me, films I'm sure she doesn't even like, to try to take my mind off my loss. She brings me books from my shelf and her shelf and the library. Eventually I feel together enough to open one. Then another. They help. I'm still in agony, but it's becoming more manageable. I can use these things – this entertainment – to temporarily take my mind off the pain. It's a month before Freya mentions work. Am I ready to go back? No, but I know I should. Freya takes me there on my first day. She doesn't ask me if I need her to, she just does it. She meets me for lunch too, and then walks me home. I don't know how she spends the time in between. I don't ask in case it makes me feel bad and I have to tell her to stop. She does this all week and on the Friday I tell her I think I'll be ok to stand on my own two feet again. And I am.

Freya never makes me talk about those days when I fell apart and she looked after me. She never makes me feel like I owe her. She never gloats. She never throws any of it back in my face. Even when she's at her lowest, calling me for help, feeling that I'm judging her, hating the life advice I am compelled to deliver as her older sister, she never lords my own mess over me. Freya kept me alive and kept me sane when I was at my lowest. She was more than just a shoulder for me, she was my whole fucking body when mine had completely failed me.

So, I guess she didn't turn out too bad after all.

A BLACK DAY

She looks different today, here. Still glowing. Still ready to be the centre of attention. Still ready to love us and leave us wanting more. But different too. Hard to say exactly how. Her outfit is perfect, but her outfit always looks perfect. I suppose, like Rob, I haven't seen her looking this dressed up for a while, or at least, not in this terribly respectable way. So, there's that. That's different. It suits her, dressing respectably. Makes her look like a serious woman on this most serious of days. Makes her look older, which I suppose could be seen as a good thing.

Her makeup is a bit much though. I want to tell her, give her a heads-up. I want to say, 'Your slap's a bit dramatic, Freya, tone it down.' But she's not close enough for a whisper and I don't want to interrupt the vicar who's saying something I can't quite hold on to. It would only make things awkward. Plus, it's too late now, I guess. This is her makeup for today.

She really does look great anyway.

A LUNCH

'Halloo,' Phil chirps as he pops his head around my open office door. 'Sian and I are off to grab lunch at that Thai place down the road. Wanna join?'

'I've got quite a lot on, Phil' I say. I know the place he means and their calamari is heavenly and incredibly reasonably priced, but I decline. 'I think I'll pick something quick up today and bring it back to my desk. Thanks though.'

'That's cool, maybe next time, ay?' he says, and as I turn back to look at my computer screen I can see in its reflection that Phil stays in the doorway a beat longer than he should, his face full of hope for a reply I don't give. I breathe a small sigh of relief when his expectant face finally disappears.

Phil started in the lab as a post-doc over nineteen months ago and he's asked me to join him for lunch at least once a week, every single week, since. Every single time I've given him a variation on the same response: 'No, Phil, I do not want to go for lunch with you.' I do not want to go for lunch with Phil because I do not want to spend my lunchbreak talking about work. Especially not with bloody Phil. I learned early on, during a quick coffee break chat, and then had it confirmed by everyone who has in fact been for lunch with him, that Phil is a young man with a passion. An earnest young man with a fire in his belly. In other words, Phil is the absolute worst.

Phil's sister killed herself when he was only sixteen and she was eighteen, and ever since he's wanted to do everything in his power to prevent others suffering what he had to suffer. That's why he chose a PhD project exploring the potential side-effects of depression medication and, after seeing a talk by yours truly at a conference in his second year, why he decided to switch his field of study to investigate suicide in model organisms. So impressed was he by my findings that he decided working in evolutionary psychology, and apparently alongside me, was the only way to truly understand what's going wrong in some people's minds so he can fix this *broken world*. Yep, that's right, it's my fault he's here. And he's over the bloody moon to be working just a few doors down from me. More than that, he seems to see me as some sort of flipping role model, someone forging the path of his crusade.

Everyone agrees Phil is incredibly annoying. Earnest people tend to be. But that's not the reason I refuse to have lunch with him. It's because I can tell he's a total carrot. Anyone can see it, he wears it on his sleeve. Life boiled him up, and now barely beneath the surface you can see his soft, vulnerable, mushy pulp. He's far too fragile to be around me. If he discovered the truth about me and my motivations, it would squish him, and I just can't stand to look into his huge, blue, admiration-filled eyes for one moment longer than I absolutely have to, knowing I'm the complete opposite of what he thinks I am. It would put me right off my calamari. So, no Phil, I do not want to go for sodding lunch with you. Take. The. Hint.

A gal's gotta eat though, so I decide to pop to the only nearby food purveyor located in the opposite direction to the delicious Thai place. I don't especially love the eatery. It's a bog-standard coffee shop with limited food options and I'm pretty sure it received a worryingly low health and safety rating recently – which now I think about it isn't really surprising given I found a small piece of cotton wool in one of their doughnuts last year – but it's worth the lunchtime sacrifice to avoid encountering any more of Phil's misplaced esteem. I have to remind myself of this value when I enter the coffee shop, as the only customer I see is a sleeping old man, leaning back on his chair, chin resting on a chest that appears to be covered in vomit. Bit alarming. I mention him to the boy at the counter, who is surely not old enough to be in employment. The boy looks over my shoulder, gives a dismissive wave of his hand, and tells me the guy's fine. Assured I've done my civic duty by alerting this unlikely-to-be-medically-trained child of the situation, I peruse the sandwich selection.

I'd really fancied one of their wraps – the duck one is surprisingly delicious if you ignore the unusual colour – but the youth informs me they're out of wraps today. Only paninis left. I'm not a huge panini fan but I'm here now and despite the faint aroma of puke in the air, I'm rather hungry. I select a chicken panini and a coffee, and when the toddler in the apron asks if I want the sandwich toasted I say no, but I assume I must have mumbled because he heads over and pops it in the panini press anyway. I'm fine with it really, it'll probably be nicer toasted, I was simply trying to rush things along. While I'm waiting, a middle-aged woman appears from a back room and joins the youngster behind the counter. She makes me my flat white and when the panini press buzzer rings she wraps the greasy bundle tightly in layers of paper, hot fat already seeping through as she turns to the café and shouts, 'Chicken pesto panini?'

I look around. It's still just me and vomit man here. I look at her and smile and nod, my hand extended. She looks me in the eye, then at my hand. She shouts 'Chicken pesto panini?' again. I say I think perhaps it might be mine. She tells me no, it's not mine. I tell her I'm pretty sure it is in fact mine. I ordered it but a few minutes ago. She repeats that no, it's not mine. I say yes, I'm fairly certain it is mine because I watched the guy I ordered and paid for it from pop it in the press, and then I watched her take the same panini out. She tells me no, I ordered the salad she's making, and she shouts the panini's name as a question again.

I see my word counts for nothing here and I must accept that. I look for the small boy, but he's disappeared, so I have no one to corroborate my story. The circumstantial evidence is surely enough though? If it's not mine then whose panini could it possibly be? Vomit guy's? I put this new argument to her. She tells me to wait for my salad. I realise we are at an impasse. My stomach growls. Maybe a salad could work? What kind of salad is it, I ask. The one you ordered, she replies. Maybe you should make it now, the salad, I suggest. Not until someone's picked up this panini, she asserts. I'm midway through humbly offering to take it off her hands if it will help, when no fewer than seven new customers crash through the door together. I don't recognise the language they're speaking very loudly, and the two youngest ones are blowing on horns, running around the small shop, and clapping their hands. The noise awakens vomit guy and he starts muttering under his breath, adding to the sudden cacophony, wafting the scent of sick with every word. Clearly agitated, the café woman puts the panini on top of the panini press and heads to serve the new customers. I spot my chance. I lean over the counter as far as I can, but I still can't quite reach my panini. I hoist myself up on to the counter for a bit of extra stretch and as I do the pre-teen returns from the back room, knocking me with the door, causing me to lose balance. I catch myself so I'm now in a sort of clumsy handstand, my hands on the floor and my legs resting on the counter. He asks what I'm doing. I say I'm trying to get my panini. He says I should have just asked for it. Great idea, I say. He attempts to pass it to me, but my hands are a little busy supporting my weight. He catches on and proceeds to help me up. Given that I weigh twice as much as he does, we work together with great difficulty and little grace. When I'm finally in an upright position we stand facing each other out of breath. He looks at me quizzically for a while, apparently wondering what I'm waiting for. I point behind him to my panini. He nods and passes it over. I nod back, take it, and leave. As I close the door behind me, I hear his colleague shout at him for giving the panini to the wrong person. I puff out my chest at the victory.

I walk back to my office, panini in hand, and I think, did that really just happen? My sore wrists suggest yes, I did actually do a handstand up against a café counter. But no one was there to see it. No one who mattered anyway. Perhaps it's just me but I find if an experience isn't shared, especially an experience as bizarre as that one, it doesn't feel truly real. It's not real until I have someone to tell it to. It's not funny until someone is laughing with me. I think that this is exactly the kind of ridiculous occurrence I would have loved telling Jamie about. Other people interrupt stories, especially strange ones, but not Jamie. She gives you her full attention and she lets you know her silence doesn't mean she's not engaged. You can see her getting more and more excited as a story builds, her head nodding, her fists clenching, her eyes widening, mouth opening. She's such a pleasure to orate to. Her reaction always validates your experience, and your feelings about it.

Jamie would have lost her actual shit at this café fiasco. She would have laughed so hard, in that deep guttural belly laugh way you can only laugh when you're completely and utterly at ease with yourself and the company you keep. It might have even topped the time I told her about my friend Hannah's car door falling off on our teenage road trip to Bournemouth. It fell clean off. Like one minute it was on the car, the next minute Hannah opened the door and it was on the floor. We had to drive all the way back to London with electrical tape holding it in place. The motorway was terrifying. And Hannah kept the car that way for years. Literally years of her crawling into the driver's seat from the passenger side, keeping her fingers crossed that the door would stay in place for long enough to pass another MOT. I guess when I told Jamie the story I told it better than I did here. Or maybe it was just the alcohol. Because I told her when we were drunkenly stumbling back home after a big night out, and it was raining, and I could see her getting more and more excited with every detail I gave, and she had turned to face me to take it all in, eyes fixed on mine, walking sideways, trusting me to guide us home. And then when she couldn't take it anymore she dropped to the wet floor in hysterical laughter. Her legs just gave way beneath her. And I dropped down laughing next to her, trying to catch my breath as I realised anew how hilarious that trip had been, catching her infectious hysterics. Then all of a sudden she stopped laughing. Her face became serious. I asked her what was wrong, loving her beautiful brown eyes, with raindrops and tears collecting on her long lashes. She looked at me solemnly and said, 'I'm peeing. I'm peeing right now. I'm wetting myself.' And we both started up again in hysterics as the rain covered up the worst of her crime.

I would love to tell her this new corker. So just for a moment, as I turn into the road my office is on, I allow myself to imagine what it would be like, to tell Jamie. I could simply take out my phone now and dial her number – which I can still recite by heart – and hear her voice and tell her what happened to me today on my lunchbreak. I could listen for the anticipation in her voice as the story built, listen for the glee as it became increasingly ridiculous, listen for the note of concern at the bit where I fell, the relief at knowing I caught myself, that this story was a happy one, a funny one. And her delight, her horror, her disbelief, her sympathy, it would all make me feel seen, understood. It would make me, and the events of my life, feel real and acknowledged. And I would love her for that. And she would love me too.

And then I pass a woman grappling with a baby who's dropped its dummy and managed to wriggle its arms free from the restraints of a pushchair. The child's screams cut through my thoughts, but the woman, who is even closer to those grating decibels, doesn't seem too perturbed. She picks up the dummy from the pavement, pops it in her own mouth for a moment – gross – and returns it to the baby's mouth, thankfully corking the wails inside. She then strokes the baby's sparse hair with one hand, soothing it sufficiently for it to allow her to place its now floppy and pliable arms back inside the buggy's harnesses. The baby locks eyes with me for a moment and I wonder if it can tell I'm not quite right. Are babies better at seeing it than others? Like the way they can see ghosts and sense evil?

The woman stands there stroking the baby's head, her frazzled and exhausted look beginning to dissipate. And now, with the baby asleep and quiet, with her hand moving so tenderly across its face, the mother looks serene, happy. Then the moment is finished, and she strolls on, and I'm reminded I won't be telling my new ridiculous story to Jamie. So, I call Freya instead, partly to check in on her. She seems to be doing well today. I walk around the block eating my panini and telling Freya about its provenance. She interrupts several times with questions, but she also laughs, and tells me about a time she slept with someone and stayed at their house and left for work in the morning and only when she went to a café loo at lunchtime did she notice she had dried sick in her hair from a tactical vomit in the club the night before. She was the café vomit guy. She says it's the first time she's ever told anyone that story. And there on the phone we make each other feel real.

A FEELING

Three weeks later and I'm at my mum's house having tea. Rob is out. Or maybe he's not. Who can say? After the normal medical appointment updates from her, and work updates from me, my mum boldly asks if I ever see Jamie nowadays, and if it's definitely, *definitely* over. I'm a little taken aback. This isn't something my mum has previously shown much interest in, not enough to raise the subject unprompted at least, and Jamie and I have been apart for nearly two years now. Can that be right? Nearly two years? It feels like half the time, although that's probably because after my first few weeks as a complete and utter wreck, I spent the rest of that first year on autopilot, constantly surprised it wasn't still the January in which we ended, shocked when birthdays and Spring and Summer and then Winter and Christmas arrived. Shocked that the world was still spinning.

I ask my mum where this is all coming from and if she's been speaking to Freya. She tells me that yes, as it happens, she has. Freya's in Greece at the moment, having taken out a loan to travel around Europe and visit refugee camps to *do her bit*. She's been making noises about heading out there since the refugee crisis began, but this time she's really gone. Except so far it seems she hasn't made it past the tourist beaches. But yes, my mum tells me they've had a chat on the phone and although they don't agree on much, they do agree Jamie was the nicest girl I'd ever introduced them to, and they'd simply like to know what she did that was so wrong that I ended it.

It wasn't Jamie, it was me, I tell her. Again. But my mum clearly doesn't want to let this go, so she asks if I still miss Jamie, if I still think about her, if I was sure about the breakup, how I knew I was sure, if the breakup still affects me now, because I don't seem to be trying to move on at all, or maybe I am moving on and just not telling my silly old mum because what does she know, and of course I'm not getting any younger so if I'm not thinking of moving on then I probably should be, and that I can speak with her if I ever I need to, and that her friend from volunteering has a daughter who isn't gay per se or not officially anyway but my mum's seen a picture of her and she has short hair and seems to play a lot of sports and has been single for a while so she might possibly be interested.

I really don't want to chat about this with my mum, not now at least, not without prior warning. I have to mentally prepare myself whenever I'm going to talk about Jamie. So much so that I've left all social media and let relationships with our mutual friends disintegrate to avoid dealing with the torture of seeing or discussing her. Because, I think to myself, still shocked by the line of questioning, yes sure Mum, the breakup still affects me. I'm only human, and Jamie was…well, Jamie was Jamie, so of course losing her still affects me. Massively. Constantly. But, I remind myself, I've been taking great strides in the right direction. For instance, when Jamie and I first parted ways I couldn't listen to music. Like, *any* music. I couldn't listen to sad songs because they were sad and I was sad, or happy songs because they were happy and I was not. I couldn't listen to songs about heartbreak because I was heartbroken, or songs about love because I'd lost it. I couldn't listen to songs that *weren't* about love or heartbreak because they seemed to be the only things in life that mattered. I couldn't listen to music I'd listened to with Jamie, or music I knew for certain Jamie liked, or music I suspected Jamie would like, or, conversely, music I knew Jamie didn't like, or music I suspected she wouldn't like if she heard it. I couldn't listen to music containing the sounds of guitars or pianos because Jamie played the guitar, and the first time I'd seen a grand piano up close had been in Jamie's aunt's home. I couldn't listen to music from the '80s because Jamie was being born in the '80s, or music from the '90s because Jamie was coming of age in the '90s, or music from the '00s because Jamie was at university in the '00s, or music from the teens because the teens was the decade that contained my happiness with Jamie, and my devastation without her.

So yeah, at first I couldn't listen to any music but after about a year and a half, so a few months ago, while I was picking up a Chinese takeaway, I happened upon a Chinese rap song that I could sit through and tap my feet to without welling up or wanting to punch myself in the ears. It's generally upbeat without being obviously happy, and I have no idea what's being said. I Shazzammed it and now I'm able to listen to that one Chinese rap song on repeat on my commute to work, which has really brightened up the journey. I feel certain in time I'll find other Chinese rap songs that'll work for me too. So, yeah, I think to myself, I'm doing ok, I've made real progress of late. But I don't tell my mum any of this because she probably wouldn't get it. Instead, I ask if we can talk about something else. Her second choice is nearly as annoying, but far more predictable at least.

My mum asks me how my dad's doing. She always asks this as though she couldn't possibly have any idea herself. Yet she knows full well how he is because she calls him a couple of times a week, visits him a couple of times a month, often cooks his favourite foods for me to take to him and even stands in for me as carer on the rare occasions I have other plans. If Jamie was puzzled by my continued contact with my dad, I'm absolutely flabbergasted by my mum's. She has never completely cut him off, even in the years directly following the divorce when he would frequently phone the house to shout abuse at her and blame her for all his problems, or show up on her doorstep at night to deliver his message in person. She would still invite him around at Christmas and Easter, no matter how disastrously it always ended, still send him a text if she hadn't heard from him for a while, still write him birthday and

Christmas and Father's Day cards, still berate my siblings and me for not seeing him enough. I usually refrain from being a broken record about it but she's got me a little riled up after blindsiding me with the Jamie quiz, so today I pick at the scab.

'*You* tell *me* how he is. I'm sure you've spoken to him more than I have.' I say, accusatorily.

'Yes,' she replies, deliberately ignoring my tone, 'I spoke with him last night and the night before and he seems to be ok. His hip's hurting but he says he's fine. As nice as it is, I'm sure it must get lonely for him in that place. But he doesn't like being *fussed* over of course.'

'So why do you fuss?'

'I don't *fuss*. I just check in to see if he's ok. I don't like the thought of him suffering there all alone.'

Why *do* we fuss? My mum spent the majority of her life – what should have been her best years – *fussing* over him. Although *fussing* doesn't quite do it justice. It was work, a full-time job alongside her actual full-time job. When she wasn't doing the hard labour of raising their children, maintaining their home, keeping in contact with his family for him and walking on eggshells to ensure he wasn't too depressed or upset or slighted by anything she, or we, said or did, she was doing the labour of being his emotional – and occasionally literal – punching bag. So maybe it's simply out of deeply ingrained habit that, even after he can no longer be legally or morally considered any of her responsibility, she is still doing that labour, that fussing. Naturally, after we found out he was ill, she's been reaching out even more. I've told her repeatedly that she doesn't *owe* him her time or her consideration or her sympathy. She doesn't owe him anything. But my mum is a pretty nice person I guess and my dad is a man she once loved very deeply. Perhaps that's all there is to it then, she's being a saint in tribute to the good ol' days, even though only a handful of them were actually any good.

But what about me? I don't consider myself a particularly caring person, but maybe all I can be is what I have seen. Maybe I'm on autopilot, doing as my mother – my role model – does. And maybe she fusses because she saw her mother fuss before her. And maybe that's because she and I and all of us have been completely duped into doing what society demands of us: looking after men, even when they've behaved horrifically. Too strong? Perhaps. But I don't see anyone, apart from Jamie and Freya, rushing to tell *me* I don't owe him anything. And I *certainly* don't see anyone expecting my brother to lift a finger to help my dad. So perhaps there's something in it. Or maybe it's not that – not for me at least. Maybe I do my *duty* because I know if I don't, yet more labour will fall to my mum, and I won't allow that. Whatever the reason, I know my mum's only trying to help, so I drop the subject and stop being so snippy.

A while later we're watching a terrible film about a man whose child has passed away. He keeps seeing flashbacks of the child and every time we see the child my mum comments that I had a pair of dungarees just like that when I was little. At the end of the film she won't let the dungarees thing go, asking if I remember them, insisting that I must. As I can't, she heads out to the garage to fetch a photo album she thinks may contain a picture of them. I shout after her that she'll never find it in all that junk, the garage being an even worse hoarder's paradise than the main house, but she ignores me. I'm surprised when she returns in only five minutes and tells me there's a method to her madness, she knows where everything is and she fully intends to get rid of most of it, she's just working her way through it bit by bit. She's been saying that for years. Here, she says, and opens it to a picture of me indeed wearing a pair of very similar flowery dungarees. I must be about five or six years old in the picture, my hair is dark but still fine, long before puberty left its frizzy wake on it. I'm on my dad's lap, beaming at the camera. He's very thin and is also smiling. Although his smile seems familiarly strained and empty, mine is totally genuine.

'Look at you, so happy there on your dad's lap,' my mum says. 'He was always your favourite of course.'

'What?' I ask, probably too aggressively. 'Are you trying to do a funny joke? Are you being sarcastic and just getting the tone wrong again?

You're obviously my favourite by a long shot, and that's not even a compliment!' I laugh, trying to take the anger out of my voice, trying to make my reaction seem light-hearted.

She laughs too, because it's true. But then she says, 'No. Of course *now* I'm your favourite, I know that, and we all know that doesn't mean much. But don't you remember how you doted on him? How he was the best dad ever? How you wished you could spend more time with him? How you did all those little drawings for him and wrote him all those sweet little notes? It would make me jealous actually, although that's a silly thing to say, but it did a bit. I was happy for him too though, and for myself I suppose, as I don't think he could have handled me being the favourite.'

The thought of this makes me embarrassed at a deeper level than the normal looking-back-at-old-pictures-of-me embarrassment. I turn the page and find a picture of myself with my mum's parents and use that to move her onto another topic.

On my ride home, as I watch the rain fall against the bus windows, I think about this idea again, that my dad was my favourite. And I remember something. I remember being walked somewhere, I don't remember where we were going, and I'm holding someone's hand as we walk along the street and I'm kicking puddles and I'm lost in my own imagination. And I remember this was a frequent imagining I'm lost in, something I would often fantasise about. I'm imagining that it's just me and my dad living together. That I don't have a mum, because when Mum's there I have to do cleaning and reading and there are always fights and she takes my dad away from me. And my dad is much cooler and nicer than my mum because he gives me the sweets I want and he wears cooler clothes and plays with me more and listens to music with me and he rarely goes to boring work during the daytime, which I know is boring because my mum has taken me to her work once and I was so bored and she basically just ignored me all day. I love him so much and I really just wish it was him and me more than anything. I don't imagine my mum has died or anything, that seems a tad harsh, but I imagine that she maybe turns out somehow not to be my real mum, that there's been some mistake and actually it turns out I only have a dad, so I get to just live with him forever and he lets me never go to school and we just play and eat sweets all the time.

I suppose this isn't exactly shocking news to me. I know full well I used to really quite like my dad when I was a child. I just don't often tend to give it much thought. In fact, the only time I ever have cause to remember it is when I am posed a stroke-of-genius question like: 'Do you think maybe you're a huge gay because your dad was such a huge prick?' It's sort of a basic question, right? But people invariably ask me as though they're having a eureka moment, as though I couldn't possibly have already considered it myself, as though I should thank them for the gift of their extraordinarily astute insight. On the contrary, this question usually makes my blood boil. It provokes a knee-jerk reaction compelling me to jump to the defence of my sexuality. It makes me want to scream: 'Who the fuck cares what caused it? I'm gay, ok? Why are you pushing your compulsory heterosexuality onto me? Why are you searching for the reason a good normal straight human has veered off course into gaytown? Why does the *why* matter so much to you? What are you going to do with that *why?* Why the fuck are *you* straight? Why do you feel the need to explain away my sexual preference? Why are you linking my entirely valid way of life to something negative and harmful? Why don't you just fuck the hell off and let me live in gaytown in peace?'

Thus far though I've always managed to bite my tongue for long enough to let this overly emotional reflex pass. And, of course, to recognise how utterly hypocritical any such outburst would be, given my whole career has been built on exploring the *why* underlying people's behaviour. Instead, I tell the smug questioner that, sure, my dad certainly wasn't a persuasive advert for selecting men as life partners, and that yeah, there's actually a fair bit of evidence suggesting LGBTQ+ people are more likely to report experiencing childhood abuse than heterosexuals. So, ok, maybe there's something to their genius theory. Maybe they've solved the puzzle of me. Maybe I'm really that simple.

Although I'm always keen to slip in that knowing the reason doesn't change the outcome; I'm a gay through and through, and indeed I'm happy with that fact. But I also tell them the jury is still out on the reason for the correlation between sexual orientation and abuse. Researchers are still asking themselves what came first, the chicken or the egg? Are you gay because you were abused, or were you abused because you are gay? Researchers aren't even completely certain more abuse has actually been suffered, wondering if people who've already stigmatised themselves by coming out as queer are simply more willing to identify as an abuse survivor than people who are still firmly part of society's in-group.

I also tell them that even though there's currently no way to know for sure what made me gay, their rather *obvious* theory just doesn't sit right with me. I'm one of those gays who's always known I was gay. Even when I was young enough for there to be no sexual element to it, my attraction has always been to women. So, I'd put my money on the born-this-way option. But if they're really keen to find environmental influences that might have helped guide me along the path to queerville, they may be looking in the wrong place. I assure them that back when my attraction to women first emerged, I was actually the leader of my father's fan club. I don't want to get into dissecting it too much because, I remind them, I'm pleased as punch with the outcome and so I'm not sure what it would achieve. But if they really must know, I spent a lot of time with my dad in my youth. I loved and admired him. So, if anything, my closeness with him and my desire to be just like him may offer more of an explanation for my youthful tomboy ways and adult homosexuality than the disdain for him I later developed.

So, yeah, I even tell people, albeit it largely only people who ask inappropriate questions, that I used to like my dad, but I rarely properly remember it and I almost never truly *feel* it. This feeling takes me by surprise. And it hits me that this feeling is the feeling of the good ol' days, and that maybe my continued contact with my dad is somehow an ode to those long lost and almost forgotten feelings I once had towards him. But more than that, I realise those feelings are only long lost and almost forgotten because they were replaced by something else. I was once young enough to have very little understanding of what my father was actually like as a man and as a result I was filled with only love and admiration for him. If I had lost him then, when he tried to lose himself, I would have been absolutely devastated. It would likely have never occurred to me that the loss was really a gain, and I would have carried that loss with me my entire life. On the plus side, I could have gone through life believing that my tragically gone-too-soon dad was nice and good. But I now *know* my father wasn't nice and good. And maybe it's just because once you know something you never want to un-know it, but I would be livid if I had been left with the impression that he was my favourite, that he was the one I would rather have kept over my mother. Maybe if he had succeeded that's how I would have felt. I might never have truly known him. Knowing him has left a hole inside me, but not knowing him might have left one too.

At least the hole I carry now is honest.

A BLACK DAY

It's quite loud now, my mum's crying. I put my arm around her and feel her body shake with every wail. People are sending a lot of sympathetic glances our way. My brother's words didn't help and I suppose she's been following what the vicar said, and perhaps it was incredibly touching. And now he, the vicar, is reading out her words, words my mum couldn't bear to say herself. So that's got to be tough for her.

Not that she'd need those prompts. It's right that she's crying, that we're all crying.

My mum doesn't ever wear makeup, and today is no exception, which means she can fully lean in to the crying. She can throw herself, make-up-less face first, into the pit of despair. I'm wearing waterproof mascara and eyeliner, but still, they're only so effective. So obviously I'm crying too, but I have to hold it in a bit. Pull myself back from the edge.

That's probably why I wore makeup today. I considered not wearing any, but the thought terrified me. I knew I would need a stupid, vain, superficial, immediate reason not to fall apart completely. A reason to have to hold it together. To have to keep things controlled. Because if I let myself go now, I don't think I'll ever come back.

A MISTAKE

My phone is making loud noises. My initial thought is my usual daily one: must be time for work, ugh. But it's still pitch black and my Ikea blackout curtains aren't *that* good. Plus, I'm pretty sure it's a Sunday. Someone must be calling me. What time is it? My alarm clock says 3am. Surely not PPI calls in the middle of the bloody night, I groggily think. Then I catch myself and realise no one calls at this hour unless they have bad news. I scramble for the phone, see it's Freya calling, and with a voice that is a mixture of panic and sleep I ask what's happened.

Freya's still in Greece. Is that why she's calling so late, I think? Time difference? But surely not, it's not that far away. Freya's hysterical, there are loud noises in the background and the signal's terrible. I try to find out where she is, who she's with, but she gives me nothing, she just wails. I finally manage to coax her into moving to a quieter area and she begins to take deep breaths and calm down. After about fifteen minutes, during which time I establish she isn't in immediate physical danger and head to the kitchen to make myself a cup of tea, Freya starts her story.

Freya absolutely positively had every intention of heading to the refugee camps to help out but first she wanted to get a feel for Greece and get insider tips on which camps to head to. So obviously she spent her first three weeks in a hostel on the beachfront in Thessaloniki, drinking and partying with kids on their gap years. She met a guy who was happy to pay for her accommodation when she couldn't afford to stay longer. He shouted her two-for-one fishbowl cocktails, MDMA, poppers – retro, I think to myself – and rides on the banana boat. What a catch. She found out about the Elaionas refugee camp in Athens and figured she could be useful there, but before going to the camp she of course had to see the sights. She met a tour guide who kindly let her stay with him and he showed her around The Parthenon and The Acropolis and The Temple of Olympian Zeus. Then she remembered that her friend Eleni from university, whom she hadn't seen in four years, and hadn't really known all that well at university anyway, lived in Athens. So she messaged Eleni on Facebook and asked if she could swing by. Eleni inexplicably agreed, and so she did indeed swing by.

It was hot when she arrived, so Freya was wearing a top that tastefully, in her opinion, showed some of her midriff. At first I'm not quite sure why Freya's thrown her outfit choice into the story, except maybe to rub it in my face, which she loves to do from time to time, that I've never had the physique to pull off a crop top. But I see its significance soon enough. Freya was welcomed into the good Greek household, where she received hugs from Eleni's mother and sister and brother and father and some people who were maybe cousins or aunts, in name if not in blood, and she was plied with aggressive amounts of food and drink. She regaled Eleni and her family with her tales of London life, her travels thus far, and her worthy intentions for Elaionas. Then Eleni's grandmother, old and doddery and plump yet withered, and dressed all in black, joined them after waking from her nap. She took a while to register that a stranger was in her midst but when she did she started speaking rapid Greek, apparently offering more food and drink and apologising for not acknowledging her before. She moved towards Freya for the traditional Greek embrace and kisses, and as Freya rose from her seat at the centre of the table the old *yiayia* became even more animated. It was *'Enkyios'* and *'moro'* and *'bravo'* and pointing at Freya, and more specifically at Freya's stomach.

Freya understood enough Greek and human body language to clock what was happening. How embarrassing, she thought. Freya had clearly gorged on their hospitality to such a degree that she'd developed a little food baby. I could imagine how she'd felt, as I feel that same wave of shame whenever a man offers me a seat on a train. Well, this outfit is going straight in the bin when I get home, is my usual thought. And that's what Freya thought about the crop top. Maybe, she pondered, she'd reached the age when, like me, she could no longer pull off a bare midriff. Except, she pointed out, it wasn't really like me, because of course I'd never been able to pull off a bare midriff. I was heartened to hear that even in her current emotionally tumultuous state she hadn't let a chance to tease me pass her by. Anyway, there she was in the house of someone she hardly knew, being congratulated on her pregnancy by an old grandma who surely must be partially sighted and perhaps have a touch of dementia to boot. How are we all going to navigate this awkward situation, she wondered, as she pulled a light shirt over her shoulders and across her stomach, as if hiding it away would make everyone forget what had just happened. It had all been said in Greek after all, so perhaps, Freya thought, she could simply pretend she hadn't understood, and the whole family could pretend to believe her. After a few moments silence that seemed like forever, during which everyone looked between Freya and the grandma and then back again, Eleni started to speak in Greek to her *yiayia*. She must be correcting and admonishing her, Freya imagined. But she imagined wrong, because Eleni next turned to her, and in plain English congratulated her. How bad Eleni had felt for not noticing before. *That* was why Freya seemed to be glowing from the moment she saw her, Eleni said, that was why her hair seemed so thick and lustrous, and her skin was so beautifully clear. Eleni's sister had the same glow each time she was pregnant and she'd had three girls, so maybe that means Freya would have a girl, the baby girl hormones coursing through her would probably be what was giving her that extra colour.

Freya didn't know what to say. Like most women, she does not respond well to being told she has a large stomach, but at the same time she couldn't cause a scene in Eleni's house after the family had been so kind to her. Plus, she had nowhere else to stay for the next few nights. So Freya simply thanked them all and claimed she was feeling a little tired and needed a nap. Eleni showed her to the room she would be staying in for the next couple of nights, and Freya, who suddenly felt genuinely incredibly tired, lay down her head and went to sleep chuckling to herself about the misunderstanding, and wondering how she was going to keep the pregnant act up for the next few days. When she awoke a few hours later it was to the sudden and terrifying realisation that perhaps it wasn't an act. Or not perhaps. Definitely. Something clicked while she was asleep, and she knew. She just knew. She hadn't had a period for months, but she hadn't thought anything of it because between her poor eating and drink and drug habits, her periods were always rather hit and miss. She'd stopped taking the pill years ago because she suspected it was contributing to her moods, but she always used protection, didn't she? It was sometimes hard to recall after a heavy night, but she thought she had. So maybe it couldn't be true. She talked herself down, laughing again at the misunderstanding, and harder this time because this crazy family had managed to not only insult her, but fool her into believing she could be pregnant too.

She kept up the act for the next couple of days, which was easier than she might have thought because heartburn had turned her off alcohol and the taboo of Freya apparently being a not only unwed but also completely un-partnered mother-to-be meant Eleni and her family waited on her hand and foot without asking too many questions. The only difficulty was convincing Eleni that a woman in her alleged state would be fine volunteering at a refugee camp. It was draining, but Freya liked that Eleni cared enough to try and stop her. She almost let Eleni persuade her, so enmeshed had she become in her story by the end of her short stay with them. But no, she had to go, although first she would go via Milos, which she had read was an island of great unspoiled beauty, although it is not actually on the way to the camps, of course. Are you getting the sense she was avoiding them? I certainly was.

Despite Milos' reputation for being untainted, Freya managed to find the tourist blemishes and found herself partying with strangers until the early hours in Adamas. On her way she had picked up a pregnancy test, well three separate testing kits actually, almost on autopilot, not thinking much of it. And one night, in a club toilet, urine flowing freely due to all the vodka sodas she had powered through her heartburn to consume, she used all three. A short wait while angry party girls banged on the door and crossed their legs, and the votes were in. It was unanimous. *Yiayia* always knows. Freya was with child.

Yet I knew this alone was not enough to warrant such hysteria. Freya was well acquainted with the morning-after pill and she'd had at least one abortion I knew of because I had been there with her. Her story continued. Freya was clear about what had to be done, even if it meant flying back to England for the procedure. But a quick google and she found she wouldn't have to fly back home, she could get what she needed easily enough in Greece. She convinced a German tourist to take her back to the mainland with him and she visited a clinic in Athens. She knew from experience how painful the procedure could be and was lamenting the days she would lose from her holiday, and of course, how she would have to wait for even longer now to offer her help at the camps. Ahem, sure. She answered the doctor's intrusive questions, she was used to those, and she wasn't shy when she was handing over her urine sample or giving her blood or pulling up her top or opening her legs to be examined. But her heart sank when the nurse and doctor started talking to one another in hushed Greek. Why were they hushing? She wouldn't have been able to understand what they were saying anyway, but she could understand hushing. Hushing meant something was wrong. And indeed it was. They instructed her to get dressed and take a seat at the desk when she was ready. Her heart was beating so loudly in her ears that at first she had to ask them to repeat themselves. Twenty-five weeks, they said again. Freya was twenty-five weeks pregnant. Her enviable stomach muscles had worked against her, holding the burgeoning new life so tightly inside her that it had more than half-formed by the time it started to show. There was no chance of getting an abortion in Greece, where the limit is twelve weeks. What about England, Freya asked? I can go back to England. I'll go back to England immediately and it will be fine. No it won't, she learned. The limit in England is twenty-four weeks.

What were you doing twenty-five weeks ago? It's tricky to remember. Freya found it difficult too. She'd assumed this person growing inside her had been made somewhere on her travels in Greece. Now she had to cast her mind back a lot further. Back to a drier spell. She thought perhaps she and that amateur drug-dealer she met at a house party had tried to hook up in the bedroom on the coats. They were very unlikely to have used protection, but she was pretty sure it hadn't worked anyway. The sex. They'd tried and failed. But maybe not. Something had succeeded. What was his name? She didn't know. She couldn't even remember the colour of his hair. Maybe she'd find out before too long, in the hair of the human she was creating. A human girl. At the clinic they had told her she would be having a girl.

It is the middle of the night and my sister is shouting and crying and screaming all of this down the phone at me. But I am wide awake and I am calm. I know what I have to do.

'I'm buying you a ticket home.' I tell her. 'You'll stay with me, both of you, until you're on your feet. This will be ok. It will all be ok.'

A BLACK DAY

It's tough to find black baby clothes. Black is apparently not the new black in babywear. There are a couple of brands that seem to specialise in cool babywear for the children of cool parents, and they do indeed use an unusually large amount of black, but their clothes are invariably too 'rock' for an occasion like today's. Little cartoon skulls wouldn't feel quite right.

We found something online in the end. A beautiful black lacy dress. It looks perfect. I wonder what the designer had in mind when they created it. A goth baby's christening? A fashionista baby's wedding-guest outfit?

Or maybe this. Maybe they had this very occasion in mind.

A NEST

There's a hell of a lot to do when you're preparing for the arrival of a new person into the world. The first thing I did when I got off the phone to Freya was sign her up for NCT classes in the local area. I now attend these with her and at the classes we largely learn about the big day, which sounds horrific, but by now I've already read two and a half incredibly frank and graphic books about pregnancy and birthing, so nothing shocks me. I'm glad someone else is there to tell Freya about it all because she doesn't listen to me and she refuses to read the books I've bought. I've had her hospital bag packed from a rather ridiculous time in advance of its use. I look through it frequently to check nothing has been forgotten.

Freya's body has been kind to her in many ways. She hasn't suffered much sickness, only a little heartburn. Of course she's noted that maybe if she *had* suffered morning sickness she'd have realised she was pregnant earlier, or at least she may not have imbibed quite so much alcohol and so many illegal substances. But she stopped all of that as soon as she found out about the pregnancy. That's what she says, and I see her every day now and I believe her. She eats the healthy food I prepare, she rests, she takes gentle exercise and her body is behaving well. We are both hoping this body kindness lasts for the birth. So far, health-wise, she is eligible for the nicest room with a pool in the birthing centre. If you try not to notice the nets resting against the wall, nets clearly used to scoop faeces out of the pool, the birthing room is like a fancy hotel suite with a jacuzzi. And although I scoffed at first, I have been accompanying her to hypnobirthing classes alongside NCT, and I think Freya may well be able to have a natural birth. Which is ironic really given the number of drugs she has ingested up until now.

In an attempt to counteract the rather hostile environment Freya had created before finding out she had a baby on board, I have stocked up on supplies to help a new human grow. There are vitamin supplements of course, folic acid and B vitamins and vitamin D and iron and all the rest. But they are no substitute for a healthy diet. I fill the fridge with protein-packed dairy products, especially live yoghurt, which has the added benefit of containing probiotics which can apparently reduce the risk of preeclampsia and vaginal infections. Freya's gone off red meat a little during the pregnancy, which is apparently very common, but I try to get her to eat it as often as possible for the protein and iron. I have finally learned to cook a few tasty lentil and chickpea dishes and I force them on Freya to fill her up with dietary folate, which will surely be processed more efficiently than the folate from the pills. I make sweet potato fries to accompany everything because Freya likes them, and because I like that they are filling her with beta-carotene that will become essential vitamin A inside her. Studies have shown that eating green leafy vegetables can reduce the risk of low birth weight and so I also top every dish off with leafy greens, which are packed full of the vitamins a pregnant woman needs. Vitamin K anyone? Who even knew there was a vitamin K? I whip up salmon dishes that will provide Freya and my growing niece with her essential fatty acids, as well as vitamin D, which I have read no one really gets enough of. That's only twice a week, mind you, because I don't want to overdose Freya and her baby with mercury. Every morning I make us eggs, with my aim of giving Freya three or four, she usually only allows two, so she can intake the requisite amount of choline with which to build a healthy new brain and nervous system. More often than not the eggs sit upon a bed of avocado on wholegrain toast, the avocado containing the good fats that make up skin and other tissues and the wholegrain for more B vitamins, fibre and magnesium. But, as they told us in NCT class, you cannot focus only on growing and birthing the baby. You have to think about life afterwards.

And so I do.

I have cooked and frozen large batches of meals, ready and waiting for when we have only the time and energy to re-heat. I have taken an intensive five-day driving course and I am now a driver. I have bought a car and although I am still terrified every time I get behind the wheel, I am becoming incrementally less so. I force myself to drive every day, with the aim of being at most half-as-terrified of driving as I was to begin with. I am making good progress. I have bought a car-seat for the baby that can face forwards and rearwards, though at first it must face rearwards, and can be adjusted in future when the baby grows into more of a proper person. I have bought a buggy that is extra thin and therefore easy to manoeuvre through London streets and public transport. It was supposed to be easy to collapse and reverse, but it took Freya and me a while to master. It is not the first buggy I bought. The first one was easy to assemble, but then I read online someone had trapped their child's finger in it and the child still had a scar, and so I returned it and bought the extra thin one I have now. I check reviews periodically to see if any young extremities have been trapped since I ordered it. I have bought muslin covered in cute animals, and nursing bras and pads to soak up boob leaks, and breast pumps and packs for freezing breast milk, and a machine that sterilises bottles and also automatically makes formula to exactly the right temperature. I have bought formula, researching which ones are closest in nutritional make-up to breast milk. Of course everyone says breast is best, but one never knows what will happen, and formula may be necessary, even from the beginning. I reassure myself with the fact that the studies showing the significant positive impact of breast milk versus formula on child development are largely those looking at old formula. New formula is surely much better? I keep my fingers crossed.

I have child-proofed my flat. This seems premature, I know, as a baby will stay very still at first, but I wanted to get it done now before all hell breaks loose. There are smooth sides and latches on doors everywhere. It's all very ugly and was terribly frustrating at first, but now I am surprised when I visit someone else's house and find I can all too easily get into a fridge or a cupboard containing dangerous liquids. I have had my carpets professionally cleaned using only the most natural hypoallergenic cleaning products and the flat is now a shoes-off space. I have bought a Moses basket and a crib and they sit alongside the bed in the spare room where Freya is staying. Freya's room. It isn't spare anymore. I bought us tickets to a make-your-own-mobile class, and we each made a mobile to be hung on top of the crib. Both of our mobiles were ugly and I didn't trust the integrity of the structures, so instead I researched the best mobiles for holding a baby's interest and stimulating development, and I bought three, which I figure we can switch between.

I have looked into toys for boosting intelligence and I now own a crate full of colourful, noisy gadgets, some soft for her first few months, then harder, spikier things, that I hope I will one day feel ok letting her play with. I find I am taken in by anything with *Baby Einstein, Baby Newton,* and suchlike in the title, which encompasses a surprisingly large range of toys. Excellent marketing. I have also signed up for the local toy library to save on landfill and I have invested in an industrial sized supply of cleaning products and baby wipes, to ensure the borrowed toys, which are shared between all the grubby babies in the local borough, are clean before they reach her.

I have hugely reduced the time I spend on my dad's care in order to minimise negativity in this coming child's life. Not being a millionaire, I can't afford to increase the amount of paid assistance he receives so I have enlisted the help of my brother. Sure, Rob complained and resisted at first, and frankly every day since, but he's stepped up and is doing a pretty good job. He's even made friends with my Dad's neighbours, people I've barely spoken to, and he's started doing errands and chores for them in exchange for a bit of cash. He still doesn't talk to any of us very much, but somehow it's in a nicer way now. Perhaps all he ever wanted was to feel needed. It hasn't escaped my notice that my mum and Freya, and all of our extended family and acquaintances, act as though Rob deserves the bloody Nobel Peace Prize for doing for only a couple of months exactly what I have been doing for a couple of years without much praise at all. I try not to dwell on this and just enjoy and appreciate Rob's help, and how far he's come.

I have invited every friend I know with kids over in order to expose both myself and Freya, when she submits to spending time with them, to their wisdom and their children. Freya tires of most people quickly, especially those with children, so she has no one to add to the list of guests with kids. I hope that through osmosis we have both become better prepared for what is to come, although the wisdom we have received is usually of the *there's nothing that can prepare you for this* variety.

I look around at my flat and my life and myself and my sister and I can see I am building something. A nest? A family? I've seen friends start families before, and of course it was completely natural for *them* to behave this way. But surely it's not natural for *me*? I've never wanted any of this, never thought this could happen. I'm not even the one who's bloody pregnant. But look at me. I've become someone I don't recognise. Until not long ago, I couldn't think of anything worse than having a child in my life, and I was grateful to be gay because it meant at least most people, most people aside from Jamie, didn't *expect* me to have a child in my life. But now? Now maybe I'm no longer simply an unwilling member of a group. Now I feel like a creator, a protector, a nurturer, an aunt? Or more? So, of course, I research this phenomenon in the evolutionary psychology literature I rely on so heavily to make sense of the world. I look into why a child-avoiding spinster like me, and specifically, a lesbian like me, might be behaving the way I am, and I find something approaching an answer. I had been distantly aware of theories for the evolution of homosexuality, but this is the first time I have decided to study it thoroughly.

Basically, the general consensus is that we gays are a puzzle indeed. Nowadays we may pop to a clinic and implant an embryo or pay for a surrogate, but when we were evolving, surely gayness should have killed us and itself off? Those of our ancestors carrying the gay genes would not have had heterosexual sex and therefore not have had babies to whom we could pass on the gay genes and rainbow flag. Now, ignoring the fact that I know very few *gold star lesbians* who have never ever had sex with a man, I can see the pull of this argument. If selection acts on reproductive power, surely we gays are the least powerful?

It turns out there are plenty of people who have tried to explain us. From my sift of Google Scholar I learn there are people who think male gay genes persist in the population because when they're carried by women they make them more fertile. It tickles me to realise how closely this resembles my friend Lara's rather inexpert theory that the fact she has two gay brothers somehow makes her hotter. There are those who propose heterozygote advantage is at play. In other words, while higher doses of a particular genetic mutation may make you a gay and reduce your chances of creating new life, medium doses give you so much of a boost in banging out babies that it cancels out the negative effects of being a bender. Or there's the theory that it is just super useful, in terms of group survival, for humans to be able to form strong bonds with people of the same sex, and sometimes those bonds are just going to be that little bit stronger than some people might like. This is strikingly similar to my mum's initial attitude to my sexuality, when she would make helpful suggestions like, maybe you simply want to be their best friend?

But the hypothesis that's relevant here, to this particular bender, me, is that of the effect of gay genes on the survival of the family unit. The idea is childless gays, like me, result in more helping hands for nieces and nephews, upping their chance of survival and of passing on some of my gay genes. And there's even a bit of real-world evidence to support it, because studies have shown gays help out with their nieces and nephews more than straights. Plus, gays tend to go into more altruistic careers, which is again some evidence that we're flipping nice helpful people.

This explains things. Doesn't it? Maybe? But I don't quite know what to do with this new information because it also comes with a new me. I have been someone who doesn't want children. I have been someone who thought I would be bad at them, with them, to them. My niece isn't even here yet but I can already sense that maybe I was wrong. Wrong to think I had to repeat my own experiences. Wrong to think the presence of a family would make me become my dad. I am more than that. I can be better than that. So, I throw myself into keeping Freya and her baby healthy and I make plans and I build a nest and I read about parenting and gay parenting and unusual families.

And all the time I think about Jamie and how maybe I was wrong about us too.

A REUNION

It's been seven months since Freya had baby *Savannah*. Don't ask me why she chose Savannah, I chose not to comment and endeavoured to keep a neutral expression when she told me. Not just Savannah though, the full name she had been endowed with was Savannah Christine Jessica Miller. Christine after our mother and Jessica after me, of course, so perhaps this placated me regarding the first name.

'Shall we just call her Jessica for short?' I had suggested.

'No' was Freya's simple response.

I was there when Savannah was born. Thirty-eight weeks, weighing 6.8lbs and with a full head of black hair. She was the most beautiful thing I had ever seen. Which just about made up for the sights that had preceded and succeeded her appearance. I really could have done without seeing any vagina go through that, and I certainly wasn't keen on it being my sister's. I averted my gaze as much as possible, parking myself firmly at the head end of the whole affair, but I couldn't stop myself staring at the placenta when it finally appeared. My god.

Truth be told, the first few weeks were a hazy hell I find difficult to believe truly happened. Vannah, as Freya had decided to call her for short, couldn't hold much milk in her tiny stomach and she needed feeding constantly day and night. Freya chose to spend those weeks wandering the flat with a feeding, crying, pooing, napping Vannah, with all the curtains drawn and in a perpetual state of undress, because what was the point of clothes? Then Freya's stitched wounds became infected and she had to be admitted to hospital for over a week. So it was my turn to seemingly endlessly wander the flat to calm Vannah, always supporting the head and using a mixture of expressed milk and formula, praying it really did have all the necessary nutrients for a growing brain. I also opted for a perpetual state of undress because who has the time to get dressed when a baby is constantly demanding something and when you will only become covered in milk and spit and vomit and urine and weird watery baby faeces anyway? I suppose we were practicing skin-to-skin parenting without even intending to. Perhaps this is how *good* parenting always happens; you muddle through in desperate terror and then attempt to apply logic afterwards to justify your choices.

Things grew steadily calmer and more manageable after Freya returned from the hospital. Vannah slept for longer and longer periods, and recently reached seven hours in one night. Freya and I both feel a little more like functioning humans as a result. Terrified of teething kicking in, I am trying my best to stockpile sleep while I can, although I'm not sure that's how sleep works. I have bought countless gels and plastic items for Savannah to gnaw on for comfort, all waiting in the fridge for when the terrible time arrives. Freya has healed well and seems to have tackled this new chapter of her life with unusual gusto. We're closer than we have ever been. Sometimes while I'm holding Savannah I catch Freya looking at me with such serenity, love, and gratitude. A few months ago she told me that she can remember now. That something about seeing me with little Vannah jogged her memory, and she can remember me looking after her, picking her up from school, making her Super Noodles and Findus Crispy Chicken pancakes, plaiting her hair and kissing her booboos. I was of course appalled, because I have vowed never to feed Savannah such processed junk – we're all organic in this household – but I was also touched. It meant a lot. I've never seen Freya so gentle and selfless as she is with Savannah. And I've never seen her so resilient and optimistic and sunny. She seems to have a sense of purpose, to know where she's going.

Savannah has changed me too. I've completely forgotten to care about work after both the university and the charity that funds my research were too progressive, or too afraid of appearing politically incorrect, to question my application for parental leave. I've put on weight through using sugar as a tool to stay awake. I have a cavity that needs filling in my back left molar because sometimes I'm just too tired to brush my teeth, and I can't remember the last time I flossed. I hardly ever wear makeup and my clothes are always dishevelled, mismatched and unclean. The lines in my forehead and around my eyes have become so deep I can no longer fool myself into thinking the next fashionable face cream will help and I wouldn't have the time to research, or the money to buy, the next fashionable face cream anyway. I constantly look like I've been shoved hastily into the same drawer as my clothes and I've had no time to iron either them or myself.

My smile lines have become even deeper through the sheer joy I feel when staring at Savannah, which makes sense, I guess. It's evolution's way of making sure we look after babies while they're at their most vulnerable, so they can carry on our genes. But knowing the science behind it doesn't lessen the pure pleasure of seeing her smile or yawn or blow a gross spit bubble. She is just like any baby anywhere, and she's not even mine, but Savannah seems to me to be the most fascinating thing I've ever seen. I watch her while she sleeps, curling her tiny hands into fists, reaching for an imaginary boob she's seeing in her dreams, and I am filled with love, and also with panic, as I obsessively check her breathing and fret about cot death. I know inside myself that I will never relax again. I will always worry about her. But I also know I will never be able to un-feel this love. It will always be in me. I will always care about her more than I do myself. I will always be less afraid of life because everything I do will have a greater purpose. I will always do anything to protect her.

Now none of this sounds like me, I know. It sounds like someone else, someone normal, someone I admire, someone I want to be. So, who am I now? The calmer past few months have allowed me not only to sleep but also to ponder this question. Am I someone new? Or have I always been this person and I just didn't recognize it before? Wasn't I cold and hard and broken and warped and full of regret and obsessed with death and suicide? Wasn't I a person who couldn't decide whether saving a life was the worst thing I'd ever done? Wasn't that who I was until Savannah came along? Or have I been telling myself the wrong story? And if I made choices based on that story, based on who I thought I was, but I was wrong about that story and myself, what about those choices? What about Jamie?

So, last week, at Freya's strong encouragement, I reached out to Jamie. I texted her and asked how she was. She replied almost instantly, which I hope is a good sign. She told me she is doing fine and that it was nice to hear from me. Hopefully another good sign? She called me *Jessie*. She was the only one who ever called me that. It felt nice. She asked how I was, and I said I was doing a whole lot better than when she last saw me. I asked if we could meet, and she said yes, that I should come over.

So I am.

Going over, that is.

Today.

To Jamie's place.

Freya's been coaching me through the meeting, helping me practice the things I want to say. For someone who's never held down a relationship for more than a few months, Freya gives startlingly good advice and I think we've worked together on something a lot less awkward than I would've come up with alone. Freya's also picked out an outfit for me. All black, and, unusually for me nowadays, actually clean. Chic even. It feels like tempting fate, but Freya said I should probably try to look nice *everywhere,* meaning that I should *groom* myself. For the first time in what feels like, and probably is, months, I shave my armpits and wax my legs and my bikini line. I make extra sure to bleach my moustache and pluck that stray black chin hair that keeps popping up.

I had my hair cut for the first time in over a year and today I fish out my makeup bag and apply eyeliner and brow pencil and concealer for my black bags. I still don't get *that* much sleep. I look in the mirror when I'm ready and I feel like the old me. But better. I feel like I'm wearing my old armour, or perhaps my old weapon, and that feels good. It gives me the confidence I need to hug Freya and Vannah, and my mum who's popped by to take Vannah to hers and give Freya some respite for a couple of hours, goodbye. And I set off for Jamie's place. Which was *our* place for a while.

I take a familiar train and tube journey and before I know it I'm in my old neighbourhood. I'm met by sights and smells that send me back to a happy time and my stomach flips at the loss. There's the old key cutters where Jamie and I looked to the future as I had my set of keys to her flat cut. There's the pizza shop where we'd stop off after a night out, where they would *always* forget to make Jamie's pizza without cheese and Jamie would seem so grateful when I'd insist they make it again properly, and I would feel like a hero. There's the repair shop, or more of a hut, where we fixed the broken screen on my phone, which although Jamie had thrown to me spectacularly well, I had even more spectacularly failed to catch.

But not everything is familiar. When I lived here Jamie and I could spend a Sunday on one of our café crawls, lazily working our way through all the hip spots in the area. Only a few years later and gentrification has progressed at such a rate as to make that impossible to achieve in a single Sunday, or maybe even a whole week. Good for Jamie, I think. I'm glad she's been living somewhere even nicer than I remember. I notice a new florist and I pop in and pick up some overpriced but gorgeous white lilies, Jamie's favourite. Carrying my bouquet I pass a new bar and I try and fail to remember what it has replaced. That makes me sad. I pass a new Japanese restaurant and I wonder whether Jamie has tried it, whether it's become one of her favourites, whether it could have been one of our favourites if I hadn't been such an absolute dickhead.

Before I know it, and before I'm ready, I'm turning into Jamie's street. My old street. And I'm getting closer to her building. My old building. And I'm walking up the stairs and I'm ringing her doorbell. My old doorbell. And I can hear movement from inside, or rather than hear it I can sort of feel it or sense it, and my heart is pounding and I'm reminded of when I used to visit her in our early days of dating and how I'd always have to wipe the sweat from my palms as I frantically tried to choose a nonchalant pose to greet her. And so I do this again. I wipe the sweat from my palms and I try to pull myself together and I lean with my left hand against the doorframe and then I decide I look like a creepy weirdo. So I stand up straight with my sweaty hands clasped behind my back like a terrified newbie soldier at attention and I'm thinking: calm down, it's only Jamie, you lived with her for four years, there's nothing to be scared of, calm down.

And she opens the door. And immediately I'm calmer. Because it's only Jamie who I lived with for four years. It's only Jamie who stroked my brow when I was sick. It's only Jamie whose breath I felt against my neck each night as I drifted off to sleep. It's only Jamie whose smile I still imagine when I find it hard to drift off alone. It's only Jamie. But as I look closer I see she's different. I have to adjust my mental image, the mental image that matches the photos of us I still regularly scroll through. Her hair is shorter, a bob. It makes her face look fuller, but in a good way. It makes her look more mature, and also more casual and laid back. She has new glasses. They're bolder than the last ones. Thicker. Blacker. She still wears all black. She still looks like a lesbian who works in a gallery, always the highest compliment I could pay her, but now maybe she's the manager, and comfortable with her position. I want to tell her this, but I don't.

'Hi Jamie. You look good.'

'Hi Jessie. You too.'

I move to protest, but then I stop myself, because she may not even be lying. Freya helped with my makeup after all and I made an extra effort to get a good night's sleep last night and my unhappiness and anxiety and reluctance to cook for one meant I had lost a great deal of weight before I put more on after Savannah's arrival, so I'm not even all that fat right now. Not properly fat, anyhow.

Jamie thanks me for the flowers, and invites me in. Seeing the flat is like seeing her. I know it, but it's changed. Spot the difference. There are things missing. Some of the missing things are in my flat, some are just gone. The photos of us, of course. The cards I'd given her that adorned our bookshelf, of course. But where's the print I bought her that used to hang above the hole in the wall where we assumed there was once a fireplace? Moved to another room? Or vanished altogether? Where's the golden lucky Chinese cat that was always on the sideboard? I never knew when she'd got it, but I liked it, and now it's elsewhere. And there are new additions. Did we buy that silver vase together? I don't think so. It's beautiful though. Jamie has impeccable taste. I'm glad we're meeting here and not at mine.

'You've finally done the kitchen,' I say, peeking at it from the living room.

'Yes, I went with the white tiles in the end,' she replies. I'd preferred the green and our deadlock was one of the reasons we'd put off the building work. I see now she was probably right.

She asks me to sit, and if I'd like a hot drink, and then she leaves me as she heads off to make me a green tea. I sit on the John Lewis sofa we agonized over and eventually bought together. I had to procure new covers after ruining the originals by putting them in the washing machine to avoid what I felt to be an extortionate dry-cleaning fee. I watch Jamie busy herself in the kitchen and I have an intense feeling of unreality, like we're both actors in a play. She's playing the dutiful host and I'm playing a new and welcome guest. But it's all for show, because we have in fact both roamed these boards before in rehearsals and on previous nights. We are as familiar as we could be yet we must pretend, for the crowd, that we hardly know each other at all. We will do this through polite conversation and tea.

'How's work?' She calls to me from the kitchen.

'Ok thanks, I'm having a bit of time off at the moment, which has been nice.'

'Oh great, yes that must be very nice.'

'And how is your work?' I ask.

'Oh, you know, it's ok. Same same. I'm looking forward to a bit of time off before long too actually.'

'Oh that'll be nice.'

All so nice.

Jamie returns with the tea and as she sets it down on the coffee table. I can smell that it's green tea with jasmine.

'Jasmine, my favourite,' I say.

And she says, 'I know.'

And we both fall awkwardly silent.

I notice she's left the teabag in my mug, which is what I used to do. At my dentist's request I stopped doing that over a year ago, to prevent the terrible teeth staining which she said gave me the appearance of a much older woman who smokes forty cigarettes a day. At her behest I also add soya milk and drink my green tea through a metal straw nowadays, but I decide not to tell Jamie. I'll tell her another time, or maybe I'll never tell her, maybe I don't need white teeth, maybe I can just go back to how I was, and how we were. I notice I'm not the only one whose habits have changed. For herself, Jamie has made a chamomile tea.

'Chamomile.' I state, without meaning to.

Her cheeks redden a little. 'I've grown to like the taste lately, maybe I'm getting old.'

There's an awkward silence and I wish I hadn't said anything, I didn't mean to embarrass her. Perhaps she's already had her four strong black coffees today, or perhaps her dentist told her they were making her look old and unhealthy too.

We talk about the pleasant weather we've been having. She tells me the garden's really coming along. I'm surprised, because we didn't do much with the small patch of earth belonging to this flat when I was here. She tells me there's a taller fence now, put up by the flat above, so the little square space feels more private. She grows herbs there.

It's very soothing, gardening, she tells me. And while Jamie's telling me about gardening and I'm chipping in with comments about the chilli plant I have on my desk which I inherited when a colleague left, and which, in truth, seems to be dying in my care, in my mind I'm re-running the words Freya and I agreed upon. The ones where I tell Jamie I'm sorry, so terribly sorry, for hurting her and for running away and hiding from what we had. I thought I was doing the right thing. I thought if she knew what was really inside of me she would run a mile, and even if she didn't I thought our children would. But I was wrong, or I'm pretty sure I wasn't entirely right at least. I have a child in my life now, and alongside Jamie, she's the best thing that's ever happened to me. I want Jamie to be part of this little unconventional family I'm building. And I want more than anything to be a parent to Jamie's children, to my own children, not only to my sister's, even though my sister's feels like my own too. Because I know now it's what I want. And more importantly, I know now I could be good at it. Or as good as the next person, which is maybe all anyone can say. I'm sorry it's taken me so long to realise it, and I'm sorry for all the pain I've caused in the process. If she has felt even half the agony I have felt over the past couple of years, then I can understand if she never forgave me. But I want us to be together forever, I want us to build a future together, and in the context of a lifetime together, I hope these few years apart will eventually melt away to nothing.

When there's a gap in the gardening chat, I muster all my courage, place my mug on the coffee table, and start in a serious tone.

'Jamie, I have something I want to say…'

'Ok Jessie, I can guess why you're here.'

I try to continue, but she won't let me.

'I would like to speak first. Please.' Jamie says as she holds up her hand against my words.

This isn't going as planned. I wanted to lay my cards out. I wanted to be open for her, to put my case to her, to give her all the evidence on which to base her decision. But she is gentle yet firm in her desire to start, and Freya and I hadn't prepared for this scenario, so I sit back and listen.

'I've been meaning to get in touch with you for a while,' she begins.

I am heartened by this, it's like fate, us both wanting to speak to each other right now. I mean, I don't believe in fate, of course, but I did once know a professor of neuroscience who believed in telepathy. All those electrical nerve signals can't be contained by the skull, he would say. Some of it must leak out. Maybe he was right. Maybe Jamie could somehow sense my shift. Maybe I could sense her desire to reach out.

'I'm sure you know I was truly heartbroken when you ended things.' Jamie continues. 'Well just broken, entirely broken, full-body inside and out broken, physically and emotionally. I couldn't function. I have never in my life felt such a deep sense of grief. I needed to understand your reasons and I just couldn't. I thought we were so in love, I was so so so so so in love…'

I nod frantically to assure her that yes, we were, I was, so in love. I am still.

'I couldn't grasp how you could walk away from that. Then living in this place was torture without you. You destroyed our life here, and just upped and left me to live amongst the ruins. Everything was a memory, every room, every book, every bloody stupid teaspoon. And it didn't stop when I left the flat. I couldn't escape you. If I saw that awful kids' cereal you would always try to eat for dinner in the supermarket, or the deodorant you used to use, or that cheap wine you always said performed above its price because someone in the shop once told you that and you thought it sounded fancy, my heart would just shatter all over again. I was like a walking wound, oozing my pain over everything around me, contaminating everything.'

'Me too,' I chime in through my frantic nodding, because it's as though she's describing my life for the past few years, but she doesn't stop, she goes on.

'I wasn't just sad Jessie, I was angry. Livid actually, livid that you could be so fucking arrogant as to make this decision apparently for *me*, apparently for *my* benefit. I was full of rage, my insides literally felt on fire with it sometimes, I could feel anger and bitterness and bile eating up every piece of me and I didn't know what to do about it. I had never felt this way before, and I couldn't see an end to it, I was scared I would always be this angry, crushed, withered shell of a person. And I swear for the first year it was like I was holding my breath. Consciously or unconsciously, I was waiting for you to come to your senses. Every text, every call, every knock at the door, I wanted it to be you regaining your marbles, changing your mind, begging for me back. But of course it was never you.'

Well huzzah! I want to scream. The day for which you have long awaited has finally arrived! For it is I, your one true love, returned to you! It was my words that flew through the sky and into your phone! It was my hand that rapped at your door! It is my lips that sip your jasmine tea, that want to sip you again. However, something in me resists the urge. Something is causing the hairs on the back of my neck to stand on end, my stomach to sink. Something in me senses a *but*...

'But...' Jamie continues, slower now, more considered, '...but then one day, after maybe fourteen months, I got a promotion at work. And I immediately text my mum and Calum and Susie who had all been so supportive, and I celebrated with the team in the naff bar across the road from the studio, and then the next day when I was having a second round of celebrations over brunch with my sister, I suddenly realised I hadn't thought about texting you with the news. Not that I actually would have texted you, you understand, but I realised I hadn't even *wanted* to tell you, or rather, I hadn't even *considered* it. At first, after you left, I had wanted to tell you everything. It was as though nothing that happened in my life was real if I hadn't shared it with you, you know?'

I knew.

'But here I was, with this big promotion, the one that you maybe remember I'd been hoping to get for ages, the one we'd discussed? And it hadn't even *occurred* to me to tell you. And when I tried, I realised I couldn't really remember the last time it had occurred to me to tell you something. And I cried, because I hadn't meant to let you go, but little by little it had happened anyway. It was shortly after that moment, that moment when I saw I had been released, that I started to see everything clearly. It felt sudden, but again, maybe it had been happening little by little. Here I was with the job I wanted, and I was moving on from you, and I was getting my life back and I should have been completely happy, but I could feel this hole inside, this hole that I think had always been there, but that our happiness partially filled in or obscured, or something. But I could feel it now, and it was growing, and I went to therapy, although I don't think I needed an expensive therapist to tell me the hole was in the shape of children, of a family. And it was like all of a sudden I could see your logic, I could get it. Now that I was no longer blinded by love.'

This punctures my heart. So her love has gone, has been gone for a while.

'I could see that everything you had said and done had been right. I'm sure you know how much that pained me, to admit you were right.'

Her joke is lost on me because I am lost right now, but I try to force a smile.

'But you were right. I saw it. And I felt freed by the knowledge, and freed by you, I guess. Freed to pursue what would fill that hole, truly fill it, because it couldn't have stayed covered forever, I would have seen it and I would have resented you. Or maybe not resented you, but I would have carried it forever, and I appreciate that you couldn't let me do that. You gave me the space to meet someone with the same-shaped hole as me, someone I could work on building the missing piece with.'

She finally pauses. I understand from the silence and from her expectant eyes that I am required to say something, but I don't quite know what. My head is spinning, and I think I must have missed something, because all I can think is that her love for me is gone. I left it too late, and her love is gone. Jamie leans back on the sofa, moving the black scarf draped around her neck aside and pulling her oversized black cashmere sweater tight around her. And then I see it. And then I get it.

'So here we are,' Jamie says, looking down and smiling. 'Here you are to congratulate me, us, and gloat about how you were right, no doubt.'

I don't manage to muster a smile this time, but she's concentrating too intently on the being in her stomach, the new love, to notice.

'Which is fine. Because you *were* right. But before you do that, I just want to say thank you. Thank you for doing what was best for me. You were always a better person than you thought you were. I told you that. But it turns out you were better than I even thought you were too. Thank you.'

My head is swimming. Maybe if I tell Jamie about my new role as an aunt, as a mum, as something in between the two, she'll find her love for me again, realise it never left, realise she's still been holding her breath and now she can exhale and we can start breathing again together, as a family this time. Maybe I haven't ruined everything? Maybe it's not too late? I feel like I'm falling. I search the room for something to ground me, something to focus on. My eyes finally rest upon a photograph on a shelf – why hadn't I seen it before? – of Jamie with her arm around a woman who doesn't look too dissimilar to me, except she's not me, of course, because she has Jamie, and seeing them together, I know I never will again. This photographic intruder looks rather pleased about the whole thing, and in the picture Jamie looks rather pleased too. They're in a field. Lavender picking perhaps? Jamie and I did that together once. Jamie is smiling so widely it somehow makes me smile too, even now. I turn to the real Jamie in front of me, looking expectantly for my reply, and I see her happiness in the flesh. I realise I'm happy too. I mean, right this minute I'm shocked and I'm broken and of course I'm devastated, but overall I realise I'm glad Jamie got what she wanted. She deserves only happiness, and I'm glad that I was instrumental in giving it to her, even if it's not in exactly the way I would have wanted.

I also realise that I'm not only happy for Jamie, I'm happy with my life. Content might be a better word. Or maybe satisfied. Sure, I'm not happy in this particular moment. Far fucking from it. I've lost Jamie, truly and forever, and the weight of that loss is almost overwhelming. But only almost. This is going to be hard. But I know I'm not going to collapse like I did the last time I lost her. Because I have a family. A *proper* family. I have

Savannah and Freya, and I have new hope that I'm better than my past and that I can build the kind of happiness Jamie's found.

'I told you so.' I finally say, and force out a laugh. 'I'm always right. Congratulations, I'm really pleased for you.'

I choose not to tell her about Savannah, it doesn't seem to make sense anymore. So we revert to small talk, and Jamie doesn't notice or pretends not to notice the new melancholy hue in my eyes, and thirty minutes later I'm standing to leave this place that used to be my home. Jamie shows me to the door and hugs me. I can feel her pregnant stomach pressing against me, and I pull her closer and breathe her in one last time.

A SUCCESS

Of course, my happiness for Jamie and my overall flowery contentedness with life doesn't stop me berating myself. My brain is full of angry rhetorical interrogators. How could I have been so wrong about who I was and what I wanted? How could I have fucked up so monumentally? And when I finally came to my senses, how could I have been so arrogant as to imagine Jamie would be sitting around for years waiting for a fuck-up like me who didn't know who I was or what I wanted? Why hadn't I woken up sooner? Why couldn't I have been the one to give her happiness? And if I'm so much flipping happier now, why does this still hurt so bloody much? Sure, I'm still walking upright this time, but why does my chest still feel as heavy as it did the first time we ended? Or heavier even? Or emptier? Like the hole is bigger? If I reckon I'm going to be so bloody ok then why is it somehow harder to breathe now that everything is out of my control, now that it's no longer my choice, and now that I know for certain this is final? Why am I always, still, forever, such a fucking loser?

These questions are the soundtrack to my journey home and as I turn my key in the lock, steeling myself to give Freya the bad news, I think I have never known such bottomless grief, and that surely this must be the worst grief I will ever feel.

I am wrong.

The house is quiet, and I remember my mum has taken Vannah for the day. I want to allow Freya to rest, so I close the kitchen door and start making myself a tea as quietly as possible. But it's no good. I pace the kitchen, repeatedly running through the conversation with Jamie in my mind and by the time the kettle's boiled I decide my brain alone can't possibly contain this much self-loathing, self-pity, and self-flagellation, so I pull down an extra mug from the shelf. Freya will need to be alert to listen to me whine. I give myself a green and Freya a Yorkshire black teabag. For almost her entire life Freya has been caffeine-free. She plied herself with all manner of illegal substances, but her body was a temple, or a Mormon church perhaps, when it came to caffeine. That was until Savannah showed up and, in Freya's words, she was so exhausted it was either start drinking tea or get far more seriously into cocaine. Now a true caffeine addict, Freya will only drink black coffee or Yorkshire tea, the latter because it's the strongest and because, as she says, people in Yorkshire know how to make a bloody good brew. I tried to inform her that research shows tea and coffee only really serve to bring a caffeine addict's level of alertness up to that of a non-addict's without caffeine, and that if I could go back in time I would choose to never get hooked in the first place. But, as she always does when I start a sentence with *research shows*, Freya told me to piss off back to the lab and play with my spiders.

I leave her teabag to stew for longer than mine and add only a touch of milk, whereas to mine I add plenty of the teeth-whiteness-protecting juice. I stir in a sweetener for Freya, leaving mine au naturale. I pick up one mug in each hand and walk towards the door, then remember I had closed the kitchen door. I try to open it with the bottom of my right hand and the base of the mug it's holding, but this proves impossible. So I turn around and, being careful not to spill any hot liquid while I do so, I make a small jumping motion, lean back against the door and then push down on the handle with my bum. It opens outwards a little quicker than I had anticipated and I lose balance slightly, but I proudly regain it without compromising either tea. This incident reminds me there will be another door to deal with at the other end, and that's why I always think I should use a tray when taking Freya some tea, however, I never remember. But today I've remembered in time. Hurray! A small win on a terrible day.

I place the mugs back on the counter and look around for the lovely William Morris print tray from the V&A. Jamie bought me that tray, and she'd had to explain to me who William Morris was on more than one occasion. He sounded like a nice guy, but I don't want to think about him or her right now, so I push that thought out of my head and continue the search. I check all the cupboards and drawers and have almost given up and convinced myself that perhaps I left the tray at Jamie's when we broke up – even though I know that can't be the case because I remember it being one of the many items I used to cry over in the first months post-breakup – when I finally spy it resting on top of one of the wall cupboards. Even on tip-toes and at full extension I can't reach it and I'm scared to jump and pull it down just in case it has something fragile resting on top that I can't see from this angle. I fetch the footstool from the living room, the footstool Freya has commandeered as a footrest for the rare moments she gets to pop her feet up, and use this to safely bring down the dusty tray. I wash it, and mindful now that the teas may be getting a little cold, I quickly load them up and begin my journey anew. I proceed only a few steps before noticing the mugs have not been sensibly placed and so I stop to address the unbalanced tray, sliding the mugs gently apart, careful not to spill the tea or let the tray go plummeting to the floor. When I'm confident I have symmetry and stability, I journey on, laughing at myself as I realise this precarious tray situation has absorbed my attention entirely and, for a few seconds at least, I haven't been thinking about Jamie. Those seconds have passed though, so I'm back to kicking myself for not being who I should have been for her, for not knowing that I actually was who I should have been for her, or both. My stomach lurches when I think of having to tell Freya that it didn't work. That she's moved on. That she's happy. That I'm happy for her. That I'm miserable about her. I know Freya will want to know exactly what was said and she'll think I didn't try hard enough.

But I'll ask her to be kind to me and I know she will be and I'll crawl into bed next to her and we'll drink tea and have sister chats like the ones we used to have when I was young and she was even younger. And when we've finished our tea I'll ask her to hug me, and she'll huff and puff and kick up a fuss because I'm such a soppy nancy, but she'll give me a hug and the human touch will hopefully induce my body to release oxytocin, dopamine and serotonin, and for a few moments maybe that will be enough to make me feel ok again.

I'm nearly at the top of the steps when the muscles in my left arm start to spasm under the weight of the tray. It's not particularly heavy but my arms have been prone to cramping lately because of the weight of lifting Savannah. On the plus side, despite having more of a tummy nowadays, my arms are more toned than they have ever been, although it doesn't feel like much of a plus when the cramps hit. The sudden movement leaves me unbalanced and as I look behind me down the stairs a wave of vertigo hits me. I run from the feeling and without breathing I race up the last few steps. At the top of the stairs I can exhale, but I still don't look back down. Instead, as I wait for the cramp to pass, my attention turns to the teas which have not come away from this last skirmish unscathed. Although the mugs are still almost full, they were previously fully-full, a mixture of green and black tea is now making patterns across the tray, almost as pretty as the William Morris flowers. I tilt the tray slightly, first this way, then that, mesmerized by the accidental beauty. An aunt on my mother's side used to read people's fortunes in the tea leaves at the bottom of their cups and I wonder what the journey of the spilled tea across this tray is saying about my fortune. I have a feeling it can't be saying anything good. It certainly seems to be indicating the tea I'll soon drink will be cold, so when my left arm is back to normal I hold the tray in both hands and pick up the momentum again.

As I turn onto the landing I'm disappointed to see Freya's door is closed. I was really hoping I wouldn't have to face any more obstacles. I walk towards it and as my hands are once again both occupied by the tray I try to knock on the door with my elbow. This might have worked if I weren't wearing a soft long-sleeved top, but the cushioning means the knock is muffled. I try again, a few times, with no reply. Although I'm unsure my left arm has sufficiently recovered, I entrust it with the whole weight of the tray and knock properly with my right hand. No reply. I look back down at the spilled tea and I'm hit by something that feels like another wave of vertigo, except I'm safe on solid ground, and when I realize what I'm feeling isn't vertigo but something more akin to déjà vu, I frantically claw at the handle and open the door.

She's lying on top of the duvet with her back to me, and I know.

Immediately I know.

But I've *known* before with Freya and I've been wrong. So I don't want to know, I still have hope.

'Freya?' I say to her back, tentatively. 'I brought you some tea.'

No response.

'Freya?' I say again, louder this time, as I walk forward past the bottom of her bed, 'It didn't go well with Jamie…wake up please…I need you.'

No response.

I'm in front of her now, looking straight on at her. She looks like she's sleeping. Maybe she's only sleeping. Except something is wrong. Her colour is wrong somehow. She's somehow too still. And what's that on the bedside table? What are all those packets, so many packets, doing there? And why have I dropped the tray and spilled the tea all over myself? And why does she feel stiff? And why isn't she moving even though I'm shaking her very hard now, too hard now. And what is that awful sound? Can't someone stop that fucking terrible sound? And why am I choking?

I step back and realize the awful guttural sound is me. I'm screaming, or wailing, or something, and I can't control it. I run downstairs, shouting no, no, no, no repeatedly on the way. I grab my mobile from my coat pocket and ring an ambulance, keeping hope alive, even though I've killed too many lab rats to know when it's too late. Then I run back upstairs, three at a time, and I start doing what I've seen people do on TV, what I vaguely remember being taught at Brownies when I was eight years old. I hold Freya's nose and breathe into her mouth. But after a while I remember that's maybe not what we're supposed to do now. I think I read somewhere we're supposed to just pump the chest now. Why didn't I sign up to be a first-aider at work? I press down on her chest with both hands hard, again and again and again, and I breathe into her mouth for good measure too, and I keep doing it again and again and again and again and again and again and again...

The ambulance arrives. And even then, even though it's been too long, I still have hope, and I race down the stairs and I let them in and I race them upstairs, and their speed and their urgency and their coordination is thrilling, and I still have hope, I still believe, even though I know, I just know, they may as well have sent a hearse. It's too late. No longer urgent in their manner. Instead, respectful and sympathetic. They confirm it for me.

It's too late.

They're sorry.

It's too late, there was nothing they could do.

They're sorry.

I stare at them blankly as they go about their work, moving Freya, being so gentle with her, for which I am grateful. They tell me some things I don't compute and they try to make me leave the room but I ignore them and carry on staring. All I can think is that it can't be true. It can't be true because I still have to tell her what happened with Jamie. She would want to hear that. I'd made her a cup of tea. She likes tea now. I was going to force her to hug me against her will. She would have wanted to hug me if I needed it.

And I really really really need it right now.

A LETTER

Mum, Jess, Savannah, Rob, I'm sorry.

I am sorry. I'm sorry.

Whenever you think of me know that I love you and imagine me saying I'm sorry to you forever because I am. None of you did anything wrong at all and none of you could have changed what happened.

I know you can't understand but I've wanted this for so long and I couldn't hold on any longer because everything always hurts too much. I went to Greece to do it in the sun and the mountains but then I found out about you Savannah and so I waited until you were in the world and big enough and I'm glad I did because you're my proudest achievement. But I still have to do this and I hope one day you'll realise you're so much better off without me around.

Thank you Jess for everything you've done. I hope things work out with Jamie you'll both make great parents. Look after Savannah she's yours too.

I love you all.

I've left lots of breast milk in the freezer.

Freya
X

A RESPONSE

The first thing I do after reading the letter I find on Freya's bedside table is wonder how she printed it. The printer has been broken for ages. Did she fix it? Did she go to the library? Or did she print this months ago? Did she break the printer printing her suicide note? She said it wasn't her, but that would be so like her to break the printer and not tell me.

The second thing I do is run downstairs and check the freezer. Freya has indeed left a *lot* of breast milk. She must have been stockpiling for weeks. How did I not notice?

The third thing I do is run to the toilet and vomit.

The fourth thing I do is ring my mum. I don't plan what to say, so when I hear her voice I panic and hang up. I should have gone to tell her in person, but that would have taken thought and it's too late now. When she rings back I have to try four times to say the thing I need to say as I pace the living room, and when it finally comes out, it's simply this: Freya's dead. She did it. She tried again and she really did it this time. We failed her.

'What?' My mum laughs. 'But we were just with her? She gave me a chocolate biscuit? A bourbon?'

'Did she?' I say. 'I didn't think we had any in. She must have bought them.'

The biscuit seems relevant somehow to us both. What does it

mean? Who buys biscuits if they're planning to kill themselves? Then my mum drops the phone, I think, I'm not sure. But she's gone for a bit and there's muffled banging and then she's back and she's screaming, she's hysterical, and everything is very loud and there's something in the background too, and I answer her questions as best I can, which is not well at all because I have no answers, and then she's gone again and I'm sure she will be coming here, though I don't think she said it, or maybe she did.

The fifth thing I do is run to the toilet and vomit again. There's nothing much in there, and my throat burns as yellow goo oozes out of me. I keep heaving even after I don't need to anymore. I want it all out. My bile. My blood. My guts. I want to be as empty as I feel. I can't do this, I can't do this, I can't do this. I can't be a person who this has happened to. I can't live this. I want to go back. Just an hour, maybe. I want to be the me who thought I was devastated, because I know now I had absolutely no clue what that meant. I want to go back to that regular innocent run-of-the-mill sadness, because by comparison it was absolute fucking bliss. This sadness is too much and I want to scream.

So I scream.

I scream until I'm sure I've broken something in my throat and I'm glad of the physical pain, I want to break every part of me by making it scream.

The sixth thing I do is think of Savannah. It should destroy me, this thought, but it doesn't. It pulls me together.

The seventh thing I do is turn on my computer and start writing this.

A MEMORY

I'm thirty-two and Freya's twenty-one. She's just struggled her way through a geography degree and I feel guilty because I remember how tough university was and I haven't spent enough time with her during her studies. I visited her in Manchester a couple of times each year but I've been so wrapped up in my research, in trying to publish and bring in more money, and in being phenomenally happy in my burgeoning relationship with Jamie, that I worry I've neglected my sister. When I express this to Jamie she suggests I take Freya away for a week over the summer, somewhere she can relax and forget about the impending results day. I hate being away from Jamie and, as co-dependent as it sounds, a week would be the longest time we've spent apart since we met. But Jamie's right, and when I invite Freya away she jumps at the chance.

I take her to the Azores because I find a cheap deal and it seems like somewhere we can avoid the lads-on-tour vibe. I do very little research into the islands, only enough to learn they're Portuguese and considered incredibly beautiful and to investigate how to travel between them. Only when I arrive at the airport do I realize how long the flight will be – it turns out the Azores are nowhere near Portugal – and how tiny the plane will be. When the plane takes off it seems to sway perilously from side to side and I grip the armrest until my knuckles shine white. Freya starts laughing at me but when she gets no response she lowers her hand onto mine and squeezes, moving closer so I feel boxed between her and the window; supported, steadied, comforted.

Being women of neither great means, nor fine taste, we are both more than satisfied with our three-star accommodation and we spend the first day lounging by the pool and planning the rest of our trip. Freya makes instant friends with the woman, Malia, on the lounger next to ours, and manages to squeeze free drinks out of her to celebrate her graduation. Malia tells us she's from Hawaii and that after her homeland the Azores is the most beautiful place she's ever been. She writes us an itinerary, adjusting it accordingly when we shame-facedly tell her neither of us can drive. She cajoles us into agreeing to join her on road trips she's planning with her husband and two daughters in their huge rental car and takes us to the hotel reception to help book us onto group tours for the other must-see destinations.

We are not disappointed. We admire views over green rolling hills while standing on dormant volcanoes. We dig our bare feet into hot black sand and watch water lapping at the coast. We see the earth drop below us from cars and tour buses as we climb lush mountains to reach waterfalls and bathe in natural springs. We feast on admittedly rather bland but still exciting food that has been buried underground and cooked only by the heat of the earth. This last-minute holiday turns out to be the best experience of our lives. Freya thanks me again and again, asking how I knew the Azores would be so beautiful. I am honest and tell her it was a fluke, but I can tell she doesn't believe me, she thinks her hero of an older sister is being modest and so I start to play up to it, to hint that I had planned it this way all along.

The tour buses are fun and well organised and they allow Freya and me to have quality time together, but we both surprise ourselves by enjoying the days with Malia and her family more. Malia treats us as one of her own, including us in the family holiday snaps and making the exact same packed lunches for us as for her husband and daughters. Strange that in only a few years, even after suspecting their significance in incredibly significant events, I will be unable to recall the names of this husband and these daughters. They simply belong to Malia. One of the daughters is in her mid-twenties and brings every conversation back to her recent engagement, which although it doesn't sound it, is rather adorable. The other is Freya's age and going into her final year of studying dance, which again, may sound annoying, but for some reason it isn't, and neither is she. The family glows with sunshine and relaxation and happiness, and I begin to think Freya and I are glowing too, reflecting their light.

One evening Malia insists we head out to dinner with them. They take us to one of the most luxurious places I've ever eaten, a training ground for silver service waiters, where the food arrives in exquisitely, and initially worryingly, tiny portions, but somehow fills us up perfectly. Malia and her husband assure us dinner is their treat and they keep the wine flowing. I'm having fun, but I realise I'm on edge. Something is stirring in the pit of my stomach and the feeling increases with each bottle of wine we put away. It dawns on me, of course, that it's the family scene that's making me so uncomfortable. Much the same thing used to happen when I was first getting to know Jamie's family. We're here with Malia, her husband and their two children, and they are drinking heavily, all of them, even the father. We're all having laughs and japes and smiles and we're sharing and learning and growing, and I am nervous. Very, very nervous. I'm waiting for it all to go wrong. I'm waiting for the warm cosy glow to ignite into something violent and ugly. I'm waiting for someone to become my dad.

'If you girls don't mind me asking, you've mentioned your mother a lot, what about your father?' Malia asks.

My filter fails and I honestly reply, 'Our parents are divorced, which was the best thing that could have happened because my dad isn't a nice person to be married to.'

There's a silence. Freya flashes me a glare I read as, *why are you ruining this for me? Why can't you just pretend to be normal?*

The family look around at each other, and then Malia sighs. She apologises. She tells me I don't have to talk about it if I don't want to –

and I don't want to – but she tells me she understands. She tells me she once had a husband like that, the girls' father. He wasn't a nice person but it was because he was very troubled. He was ill. She tells me her husband who sits with us now – she probably uses his name, but I'll still never remember it – is the girls' stepfather, but as he had a far greater hand in raising them than their biological father, they both call him Dad. She tells me their biological father – and I notice Malia lowers her voice when she speaks about him – walked out on them when the girls were only two and five years old. She clearly doesn't want to badmouth him too much in front of his children, but she repeats that he was very troubled and says everything happens for a reason, while squeezing her apparently untroubled husband's hand. Athough she doesn't say it, I can see that clearly Malia feels this has all worked out for the best, she seems happy with her life, happy with her kind gentle husband and her family holidays and her enjoyable boozy family dinners. She seems happy her daughters can glow, and surely they wouldn't have glowed as brightly with their *troubled* father at the table? And as she moves onto a more palatable topic she gives me a sympathetic look, a look which seems to say she's sorry Freya and I may never be able to glow like her girls. The look passes in an instant, and perhaps it never happened at all, perhaps it's just the wine, but when we say our goodbyes at the end of the evening Malia hugs me extra close and I'm sure it did happen. The look.

When we get back to the room, both rather inebriated, my mind is racing. I lie in bed staring at the ceiling. I contemplate calling across the room to Freya.

'Why did you do that?' she says at that exact moment, as if she can read my thoughts.

'Do what?'

'Bring up Dad at dinner? So awkward!'

I remind Freya I didn't actually bring him up, Malia did, I simply answered her question. 'You know what I mean,' Freya says, exasperated.

'Yes, I know.'

There's a silence. I don't know how to fill it.

'I'm drunk,' I say, because I'm drunk.

'Me too,' she says.

'I guess that's why I spoke about Dad. Because I'm drunk.'

'And because you're so weirdly obsessed with him.' Freya laughs.

This again. She can't understand why I still see him, why I treat him as though he's something other than a figure of hate to me, even though this is before I start having to see him regularly and cook and clean for him, which she'll understand even less. Why can't I just cut him out completely like she has? Why, indeed.

'It's interesting, what Malia said about the girls' dad.'

'Yeah, I totally thought her husband was their dad, right? I guess he is a bit too blonde and tall though. Lucky her twat of a first husband left. Otherwise she might never have met that lovely guy, and they might never have bought us such a lush dinner!' Freya chuckles to herself.

I don't feel too good. I should go to sleep but I'm drunk, like head-swimmingly drunk. How much wine did we drink? Instead I take this moment, here in the dark, to tell Freya about our father's failed attempt to leave us. She is completely silent as I tell her about the memory that still haunts me, our pregnant mum's request, my treacherous tea climb, my shock finding at the summit, my life-saving sounding of the alarm. She's so silent that when I finish I think maybe she's fallen asleep, and I think maybe that would be best as I hadn't planned to tell her that story ever, let alone on a celebratory holiday. In the silence I am suddenly exhausted and I'm almost asleep myself.

'You should have let him die.' Freya says very quietly and seriously. 'It would have been better for everyone.'

'I think so too sometimes,' I slur groggily, already half in a dream, 'but if I'd done that, you would never have existed. So, it doesn't work, that logic. It never works.'

'Maybe that would have been ok.' I think I hear her whisper, and then before I can respond she says, 'or maybe I would have existed, somehow, but I would have been better. We all would have been better. You should have let him.'

'I'm sorry,' I say, before giving in completely to sleep.

The next morning my mouth is furry and my head hurts. But that sort of feels like a blessing because the alcoholic haze and pitch black in which our bedroom chat occurred gives it an unreal quality, and it feels as though our conversation the night before never happened at all. We pass the final few days of the holiday much like the first, enjoying the views, the sun, the food and the drink, largely in the company of Malia and her beautiful family. When it's time to leave, Freya and I are truly gutted. We joke about extending our stay, about buying a tent and camping on the beach if we can't afford the room, about ditching our life in England and setting up a café here, where all of the cakes would be baked using the heat of the earth so we wouldn't have to pay for fuel. But we pack, and we order our taxi to the airport, and we get into that taxi when it arrives, and from there we check our bags and get into the plane. When it's time to board and I see the teeny tiny plane again, it adds an edge of fear to the sadness of returning to normal life. Although the weather is lovely today, it's quite windy, and as we ascend, the familiar shaking occurs. I remember reading that take-off and landing are the most dangerous parts of any plane journey and my knuckles are white again as I grip the arm rests. Freya is even calmer this time.

'Don't worry' she says as she places her hand over mine, 'I love you sis. We had such a lovely time. Thank you so much. It'll be alright if it happens now. It'll even be best.'

I think that's what she says. I'm so terrified and the engine is making such a loud noise and I have earplugs in and I am chewing gum aggressively to avoid my ears popping, so I'm not quite sure I hear her properly.

A BLACK DAY

I'm vaguely aware of people looking at me expectantly. My mum's nudging me. She's been a complete mess, but she's also been keeping up with things in a way I have not. It's your turn, she tells me. My turn. I don't have to do it if I don't want to, she says. My mum knew she wouldn't be able to do it. I wasn't so sure, so I've given the vicar – Rupert, a nice man, very understanding about just how un-religious we are, promising he could be religious enough for us all – my reading, and told him I'll give him the nod if I can't handle it.

I want to be able to handle it. It feels important somehow. As if this will set the tone for everything that comes next. I must step up.

I wander to the front. I feel like I'm gliding. Like my brain is tethered extremely loosely to my body. I can command its movements, but only just. I concentrate my full attention on not tripping up the steps, and it works. I don't trip. I glance over at the open casket and notice, or perhaps only imagine, what seems to be the slightest of supportive smiles on Freya's unusually calm face. Rupert-the-vicar asks quietly if I'd like him to stand with me while I read. I look at him confused and he seems to take that as a no and steps back. I can feel him not too far away though. If words fail me he'll take the lead.

I look at the crowd. Literally, it's a crowd. Even living the way she did, or perhaps especially living the way she did, Freya clearly touched a good number of lives. I feel with extreme certainty that Freya brought a great deal of joy to these people, even as she experienced a deficit of joy herself. I recognise some of them – her housemates, a couple of her most recent colleagues, a few classmates I met at her university graduation – but most of them are new to me. Apart from our family, the people in front of me are overwhelmingly young and hipster-looking. I think, Freya would have liked the vibe here. Very trendy. Which makes me smile. I wish she could have known how many trendy people valued her life. This thought summons the tears again. I can't have that right now, so I push them back down. I steel myself and, rather robotically, I read my reading.

'Everyone must leave something behind when he dies, my grandfather said. A child or a book or a painting or a house or a wall built or a pair of shoes made. Or a garden planted. Something your hand touched some way so your soul has somewhere to go when you die, and when people look at that tree or that flower you planted, you're there. It doesn't matter what you do, he said, so long as you change something from the way it was before you touched it into something that's like you after you take your hands away.'

I found the reading in a blog list of top-ten non-religious funeral readings. Which seems lame. But it doesn't feel lame. It's from Ray Bradbury's Fahrenheit 451, a book we read in our book group a while ago. Freya said she was going to read it and attend the meeting, but of course she did neither. I remember this passage struck me as poignant even at the time. I should have shared it with her before now.

I have more I want to say to the crowd, more than just this reading. I want to tell people what this passage means to me, why it spoke to me, but I can only manage to share someone else's words today, not my own. I worry the young hip people in the crowd won't understand what I'm getting at though. Freya never built a wall or a house or a pair of shoes. Surely nowadays very few of us have? She probably never even did a painting, not as an adult, and she definitely didn't like gardening. She never had a garden of her own, for one thing. Plus, the pace would have been far too slow for her anyway. Which is a shame really, given how therapeutic gardening is supposed to be for our mental health.

But that's not why I chose the reading, to encourage listeners to garden. I chose it because it resonated with me, because my world still looks like Freya. My world, or the most important part of it, the part sat there in the front row, reflects Freya. I find her face in all of them, just as I find it in the mirror. And right there, now in my mum's arms because she'd started fidgeting in the buggy, is the part of the world that looks most like Freya, the gift Freya left us when she took her hand away. The gift we all crowd around. The gift that's kept us going through this, that's pulled us together instead of apart. The gift I've even let my dad hold these past few weeks. Sitting her on his lap while he's rolled around in his new wheelchair. And he seems cheered by her, just as he was cheered by Freya when she let him be, just as we all were when she let us be.

I don't manage to say any of that in the church. Instead I walk back to my seat in a daze, and join everyone in mouthing the words to a hymn I must have chosen.

But I want you to know that's why I chose the reading.

A HOT DRINK

Shortly after Freya's funeral I learned I had to set myself alarms. There's an alarm to remind me to have breakfast, lunch, and dinner. There's an alarm to remind me to go to sleep. Because I was forgetting. I was focusing on you and your food and your sleep. And I was throwing myself into work. And when I wasn't focusing on you, or on work, I was focusing on this. On writing this.

What is this?

I've been writing it for ten months now, whenever I get a moment alone. I put you to bed and I write. I drop you at my mum's or the nursery, and I write. At work I take my lunch break and I write.

At some point, maybe only recently, I realised it was for you.

I've changed jobs. I had to. How could I carry on researching suicide day in day out, surreptitiously trying to prove it was often for the best, that families should be somehow grateful for it, that it was in fact on some level done for their benefit? Although I knew better than to publicise them, I was so sure of my ideas, so sure of my work, my purpose, my mission. I was the one who was going to change everything, who would defend the act and make people see the truth, a truth to help them realise they didn't have to feel sorrow or shame or regret, because evolution is working exactly as it should. I felt certain I was *built* for revealing this truth. I was sure it was my vocation, and I could never have imagined anything would make me feel differently.

It turns out I didn't have a very good imagination.

I'm sure of nothing now, so how could I continue to be what I have been? I had to change my purpose, my life. You will probably have questions about this change. Questions are only natural. Your questions will probably go something like this: Does leaving the work behind mean I think I was wrong all those years? Do I now view what happened to Adam, to Beth, to my spiders and to my father, through new eyes? Has my personal bereavement, with its accompanying unending inky trench of grief, cancelled out everything I had always believed, and precipitated a paradigm-shift? Have I joined Saints Augustine and Thomas Aquinas on the anti-suicide train? Does my sometimes furiously uncontainable anger, my white-hot burning rage at Freya for throwing her one wonderful and precious life away, leaving us to hobble on without her, mean I now agree suicide survivors should be punished? Or has guilt, heavy and harassing, turned me away from something I still know to be true? Do I maintain I was correct, but that Freya's case doesn't count? Do I feel she was a tragic anomaly, for there are always anomalies, a glitch in the otherwise sensible evolutionarily-honed suicide system? Or am I simply too cowardly to confront the possibility that I was indeed right all along, that even here and now, as we barely tread water in our ocean of loss, our family is actually better off because of what my sister, my only, beautiful, flawed, irreplaceable sister, did? And if this is true, am I not only a coward, then, but a complete and utter hypocrite to boot? Because even if my theory was right, even if it could be conclusively proven that evolutionarily this is all definitely for the best, why would I still do anything, absolutely anything, to go back, to notice she needed more help, to get there in time, to keep her with us?

These are very good questions, but all I can tell you is I'm afraid I don't know. What I do know is I can't even bear to *ask* those questions anymore, let alone try to answer them. I know it all became too close. I know that even if I still think someone should be pondering this scientific puzzle, I don't want to be that someone. I know I would rather try to be happy and sane than right.

So I switched, and it was surprisingly easy to switch. My supervisor knew someone working on homosexuality and child-rearing. She'd been wowed by studies showing children of lesbian parents do no worse, or even do better, on many emotional measures than those of non-lesbian parents. She ignored some of the possible confounders of these studies and started to search for an evolutionary basis. She's studying a range of animals, from penguins to humans, to see whether having gay parents, or gay relatives, makes for happier and healthier and more fecund offspring. If it does, it would go some way to explaining why homosexuality persists in all manner of species.

I don't know what the answer is. I don't know that I really care anymore. Or perhaps that's not true. I don't feel this is my vocation, not like before, but I know what I'd prefer the answer to be. Ultimately though, all I really care about is being able to ask a question I'm comfortable asking. A question that fills me with hope instead of despair and remorse. Now I get to play with penguins and interview humans, whom I like infinitely more than my spiders. And although I'm still struggling to hold everything together, to put one foot in front of the other, I get to try my very best to push all my heaviness away so I can bring only lightness back to you every evening.

So, what *is* this?

At first I thought it was a confession. Then I thought it was my particular form of therapy. There have been ugly times when I felt it might even be my own ridiculously long suicide note. Although I knew that would never really be the case. Because of you. Or maybe that's unfair. I knew it would never really be the case because of me. Because for some reason, probably just by chance, I don't seem to have *that* in me. I know now this thing I've been writing is for you, Savannah. I don't know if or how or when I'll give it to you – I'm pretty sure there's at least one sex bit that'll have to be removed before I do – but it's written for you.

It's a story about things that might have harmed your mum and things I know have certainly harmed me. I can't take on another story like that.

Because the clue is there in the name: it's a story. It's all a story. We decide which bits of our lives have meaning and consequence, which bits to hold on to and use as a guide. I held onto the wrong thing for too long. There's too much at stake now. I have to focus on a different version of the world and of me. Maybe I'm a natural nurturer, the altruistic one, the helper of the family, the one who ensures our genes are passed on. Like much evolutionary theory, it reeks of biased emotional bullshit. But if it's all bullshit anyway, I'm choosing the bullshit that will get me through the day.

What will get you through the day? I wonder this as you clap your hands and smile at me, as you scream with delight at colourful YouTube buffoonery, as you throw your carrots and peas across the room and laugh at my exasperation. You waddle for the first time across the seemingly endless distance between the living room chair and my open arms, and I scoop you up and throw you into the air and we celebrate, and as I wish your mum could be here to see this, I wonder, what story will you carry with you?

Sometimes I feel it's pointless, attempting to influence your story in any way. All I can do is be here for you, be loving, be consistent, be firm, be safe, be a parent, and hope for the best. Maybe that's true. But a parent does everything they can to help, even if they know they can't. So, this is me trying to influence your story, by showing you how you've influenced mine. I'm trying to show you me, and the effect you've had on me. I'm writing it down because I worry that once we know each other, these things will become harder and harder to tell you. I worry I won't know how to say all of this to the person you will become. I worry that maybe, like many families, one day it will be impossible for me to show myself to you, and impossible for you to really see me. So here I am, telling you the bit of my story that is the beginning of yours.

Your story started before anyone even knew you. The very fact of you changed everything. I can see now, more clearly than I ever have, that your mum was in a great deal of pain for a great deal of time. But she carried on for you, and only for you. She made sure you were here, alive, cared for, loved, and even in leaving, rightly or wrongly, she felt she was giving you the best of her.

And you changed things for me. I thought I was one thing for the longest time, but you showed me I am something entirely different. I use theory and empirical studies to try to explain this transformation, but that's all noise. It was you, your glorious arrival, that changed everything. Before you, I thought I was worthless. I believed a combination of my genes and my surroundings had irrevocably hardened me. Never mind the coffee beans, I used to find myself jealous of the bloody carrots, the people who'd faced life's hot water and at least retained some softness, albeit too much, because I had been boiled into nothing but a tough useless egg. And maybe before you that is all I was. But today in our kitchen, where I used to sit with your mum, I popped you in your high chair and I tried something. I bypassed the grinder and the coffee machine and I boiled some whole coffee beans in a pan. They made pretty nice coffee and the beans came out fairly firm and largely untouched, just a little darker. I poured the wet beans onto the kitchen table and stared at them for the longest time, batting your hands away as you reached for the choking hazard. I think about those coffee beans, and about my dad and your mum and Jamie, and I know I'm not there yet, I'm not one of those perfect little beans. But I'm trying. For you I'm really trying.

In the meantime, you've shown me I can be more than an egg. Maybe I can be a teabag instead of a coffee bean. A good strong teabag from Yorkshire, where they know how to make good strong proper tea. The hot water may make me saggy and soggy and sad, but for you, I'll do my best to make it into a damn good cup of tea.

ACKNOWLEDGEMENTS

Thanks to all those who didn't laugh at me, at least not out loud, when I shared I was starting to write fiction. I can't express how much your straight faces encouraged me to plough on with this. Among all the non-laughers, special thanks must go to Seán and Adam at époque press, who saw potential in my work, and whose expert eyes, gentle feedback, and saintly patience, helped improve it. Thanks to Rhiannon for reading my writing, even though it pains you, and thanks to Susanne for sharing your own progress and spurring me on. Thanks to Rosie, Lucy, Clare, my mum, and AJ; your support with this pursuit has meant the world.

Thanks to my original creative partners, Harriet and Juan, we must work together again someday. And thanks to Felicity for unwittingly setting me on this path.

Last but by no means least, thanks to my family for being my family, and to my partner for being my partner. Especially during the past few years, you have all been so important to me, and have helped me get my book (I've got a book!) out there.